Sick Darlings

Lee B Chaffee

Triggers: Voyeurism, Anal, CNC, Non-Con,

Sibling Intent/ romantic feelings, Suicide and Mentions of Suicide

Torture and torment, abduction, captive and assault.

Mental and physical abuse.

There's probably more and I am numb to them, so I don't really notice them.

ISBN: 978-1-7388469-0-0

DEDICATION

I don't know what to say anymore.

If you're related to me,
this is another book that you probably shouldn't read.

CONTENTS

ACKNOWLEDGMENTS

I want to thank my alpha, beta and arc readers!

You few have been a wonderful group who has helped this brain baby become a reality. Thank you for your continued support.

xoxo

1

Tempting Fate

Anika Darling

"I think I'm pregnant," Anika daringly mumbled to get a rise from him.

She trembled, watching Slade stand and turn to face her. He was clearly not in the most stable of states and she was stupid enough to pick that moment to goad him. Was it too much to ask for a bit of attention? Apparently, it was.

The glow from his large computer monitor barely gave off enough light for her to see his immaculately clean room. It did, however, make a halo around his tall slender frame, while darkening his features. Watching too many cryptid countdown videos must have had far more effect on her than she thought because the scene before her brought to mind horror stories of Slender Man. The way his long limbs dangled at his side and how none of his features were visible triggered some horror movie vibes for her. He made the sensation so much worse by how fast he bolted across the room toward her.

"I'm sorry!" blurted from her lips in a knee jerk reaction as her eyes snapped shut.

His icy hands snaked their way around her upper arms as he took them in a vice-like grip. They were so cold against her feverish skin that they practically burned her. Her breath caught in her throat as she tilted her head back and her eyes slowly fluttered open to take in his features. His distinctive auburn eyes were so bright they nearly looked red. They were hugged by long dark eyelashes and supported by dark bags under them from lack of sleep. His nose was bold and slightly wide, suiting his full, thick lips, which rarely pulled into a smile. When they did, he never looked very pleasant. Appearances aren't everything. He smelled like a clean mixture of his soap and cologne, which seemed to hover around him in an invisible plume.

"Anika," Slade whispered her name in a dangerous hiss that sent chills down her spine.

Why did he hate her so much?! The way he drew his dark eyebrows down over his eyes in a disdained glare. He shoved her aside, making her stumble, nearly falling. Anika grabbed the edge of his doorway to catch herself and keep from hitting the floor. His eyes didn't meet hers. Instead, they slowly trailed up and down her slight frame as if seeing right through to her soul.

Without another word, Slade stomped away, down the hall toward the kitchen. Watching his swift movements, she quivered, grabbing the edge of his doorway with both hands to keep her knees from giving way. She struggled with feeling frustrated, neglected and just a little afraid of what he would do next in his volatile state. Anika's bottom lip quivered slightly, but she pulled it into her mouth and bit hard to keep herself from crying. If she cried, and Slade saw, he'd only get mad and yell at her.

Light from the refrigerator exploded into the room ahead, trickling down the hall toward her. She finally pried her hands from the frame to wrap her arms around herself. A large part of her wanted desperately to follow him. Her hesitation was purely from fear, knowing deep down how scary and unstable he could be.

She loved and loathed her dearest brother.

2

Loved and Loathed
Slade Darling

He could barely cope with her news. It was a nasty prank, which he saw through instantly, but that didn't mean it hadn't got him thinking. The intrusive thoughts massacred his mind and made him feel like he was drowning. The more the minutes ticked by, the sicker his stomach felt, turning and writhing as if he'd been poisoned by her mere words. It was a struggle to pretend that the thought didn't haunt him as he tried to enjoy the atmosphere he had manufactured.

They sat at the table across from one another. Slade licked his dry lips as his crimson eyes traced over her small and nearly curveless body. Her breasts were bigger than they should have been, but this wide-eyed girl was, for all intents and purposes, his sweet baby sister.

Her hand trembled slightly as she scooped up a third bite of day-old linguini onto her fork. Her eyes wouldn't meet his, but he knew they would be a polar opposite of his own, dark blue. Her nose and lips were less aggressively bold than his, which only made her seem more attractive. Some features weren't exactly what he wanted, but imagination did the rest. In the past few months, her hair had grown nearly an inch, which only helped with the fantasy.

Slade applied pressure to his heels on the floor to slide his chair back from the small dinner table as he prepared to stand. The wooden legs obnoxiously scraped the basement's concrete floor, making the young woman twitch. The tremor that followed caused her fork to slip from her clumsy hand and clatter loudly onto the ceramic plate. Her reaction irked him, but that wasn't entirely out of character either. Deliberately, he slowly rose the rest of the way to his feet, basking in every anxiety-driven response she had to his presence.

His long pianist fingers dragged across the coarse tabletop, feeling each ridge and dimple. He became hyper aware of all his surroundings though his sole focus was always on the woman. Without pulling his gaze from her features, he reached out and pinched the wick on one of the two candles, extinguishing it with a hissing sizzle.

While preparing for their evening, Slade meticulously arranged the table settings to encourage a romantic ambiance. Littering the pock-marked surface between the two candles were flower petals he collected from the neighbor's garden. The scent of aromatic incense, which sent little tendrils of spiraling smoke into the air combined with bleach, tickled his nose. For the occasion, he meticulously cleaned and washed the entire basement.

He inched his way closer to her at a lingering pace. The girl's throat muscles visibly constricted as she swallowed. Her nostrils flared and eyes bulged when his knee slightly knocked one of hers.

"My love," he drawled, hoping to sound the least bit sultry.

Watching her eyes close as he came to a halt in front of her annoyed him more than it should have. He kneeled down so the only thing she'd see when she opened them was his face. Slowly, his fingers moved to her thigh, just above where his knee touched.

When he touched her, the girl tensed. The skin was so hot, practically feverish. Her little night dress only came midway up her thigh, exposing far too much skin for him to allow anyone else to lay eyes on her. His fingers trailed upward, so her knees pulled tight together. Along the divide, her skin immediately turned white from the pressure.

Pushing his hand up her thigh, he basked in the fiery heat rising from her flesh. When his fingertips reached the lacy edge of her nighty, he forced his thumb into the crevasse between her legs. Slade arched his thumb, so his nail scratched her, encouraging her to spread her thighs and accept his touch.

He purred in his throat before giving her the praise she so desperately desired. "Good girl." His lips pulled into a tight smile when her eyes fluttered open. "There you are, my shy little girl."

As if trying to set his heart aflutter, she gave him a timid, wavering smile. The silky material of her nighty tugged as his hand pursued the thing he desired. It became lax when he finally moved beneath the material, allowing him to proceed in his advance. The thin material hid his fingers from sight as they tasted that molten passion at her center.

"I need to shave this, huh?" his fingertips lightly tickled the two-week hair growth, which had gone from coarse to soft over the past few days.

"I'm thorry," her voice trembled as she mumbled a whimpering apology.

"Oh, my baby girl," he cooed, pushing the tip of his middle finger between her lips, enjoying the heat and moisture. "That's a natural part of becoming a grownup."

Her legs spread a little more for him. He was sure it had nothing to do with the fact that his sharp nail scratched her inner thigh. When he smirked, showing his approval, her knees drifted further apart until her outer thighs pressed into the arm rest supports of her chair. His precious girl clearly wanted him so badly that she encouraged his advances. Her hesitation was her own nervousness about giving her body to another.

"Oh, you naughty little girl," he chortled, pushing his fingers forward in search of her clit.

She gasped mutedly. Her hands didn't dare move from their resting place on her thighs, though they balled into fists. Her stomach muscles clenched. However, his focus was on her expression. Her jaw carried so much tension that a vein popped out just under her temple, yet her mouth was not entirely closed. Those cute little nostrils flared, and her eyes seemed to be as wide as they could go.

"I'm going to take your virginity, but-." He moved his hand forward and slipped the tip of his middle finger into the hole. "But I want to forgo the use of protection."

Her eyes widened in horror the instant before her legs clapped closed, trapping his hand like a snapdragon plant catching a fly in its sweet nectar.

Fair enough. They've always used protection, and this time should have been no different, but he couldn't get those words out of his head. He could mentally cope with her resistance, even finding it amusing. Until the tears rolled down her cheeks, he could contend with her behavior. The tears destroyed the entire façade!

Slade took an agonizing breath to combat the sharp knife-like pain radiating from his chest. It did nothing to ease the rage that made flecks of white dance across his vision. His teeth clenched hard enough he feared they'd shatter. If they did, his fiery rage was enough that he'd spit the shards in her face, then fuck it till she suffocated on his cock.

"You are ruining it, you dumb bitch!" He roared in her face, suddenly flipping from that tender, loving brother into the monster he never wanted her to witness.

His hand shot out to catch her by her matted hair. She screamed in a combination of fear and surprise, but her terror didn't slow him down. Now, he wanted to scare her; he wanted her so scared that she couldn't cry for fear of repercussions.

"Maybe you need a reminder of what will happen if you displease me, whore!"

Slade's rage was the kind that built immediately and could be set off by the slightest thing. He lacked social skills, and the other children often called him creepy when he was in school. After losing his parents, it was as if he were set free, aside from a chain by the name of Anika. His resentment toward the little girl who always had his parents' attention slowly turned into an obsession akin to love.

"I'm thorry!" the brunette shrieked in terror as he yanked her to her feet before half-dragged her across the room.

He was tall and scrawny, but had a little more strength than what seemed possible for his physique. His long limbs moved them twice as fast as she was capable of following, so she floundered about behind him with her hands helplessly clawing at the hand he had tangled in her hair. He marched her across the room toward the space under the stairs. When the stupid girl realized where they were headed, utter panic took over and her legs gave out, so clumps of hair tore from her scalp. Her hands clawed at his clothes, trying to latch onto him like the insect she was.

"Pleath!"

Under the wooden stairs were two massive white deep freezers. Hilariously, only one was used for food. The other one was used to store meat of a different kind. Slade led her to believe they both held the same thing, and he wasn't about to correct her. On the floor, coming from under the freezer, were some thick chains, and hanging on hooks above it were the other ends, attached to locks. He always made sure everything was prepared in case he needed to use it.

He used his free hand to throw open the lid. It whapped the chains above, making them rattle loudly. A blast of chilly air radiated from the freezer, making goosebumps rise across his arms and neck. The cold wasn't the only reason Slade felt queasy. The contents were unappealing.

The pathetic woman's frantic struggles became more aggressive, but were easily ignored. She had to know what was coming. This wasn't the first time he'd punished her in this way.

"No! No, pweeb!"

Her begging didn't do anything but piss him off more. He was already seething. Her tears had ruined his fantasy dinner date with her. Slade was already having trouble with his irritation and boredom. He waited half an hour for her to eat three fucking bites of food. She took her sweet ass time, drawing one moment into the next for the entire meal.

"Up we go." His tone of voice was far too cheerful for their deranged circumstances.

Scooping his victim into his arms was the simple part. Getting her to let go of him as he attempted to drop her nonchalantly into the freezer was a whole different story. Her bottom half fell in, and he grabbed her forearms to pry her hands from around the back of his neck. She didn't have far to fall, because the freezer was half-full.

The scream that erupted from her was like a symphony of unparalleled horror. He slammed the lid shut, catching her fingers along the edge, but pressed down all that much harder. He didn't give a damn if he broke her fingers. In his moment of blind rage, she was certainly nothing more than a doll to him. She screamed words, but he could clearly hear nothing through the insulated freezer.

Holding it shut with his forearm, Slade snatched up the end of the chain from the ground and attached it to the one from the hook from overhead. He linked the ends as ensuring to pull it tight as possible to ensure the freezer would stay tightly shut. He locked the chains together with a loud click that felt almost deafening.

He stepped back to admire his handy work. Another set of chains hung next to where the first had been. This time, she was weak, so there was no need for the second chain to be attached. She screamed and shrieked, hitting and kicking the lid, but it barely budged, not even enough for her to pry her fingers from where they were trapped.

Her behavior was a minor annoyance. He soothed himself mentally as he marched across the room to clean up from their dinner. Slade blew out the second candle, struggling with his rage at how she ruined their romantic dinner for two. Damn dumb bitch.

He picked up their dishes, stacking them before carrying them toward the stairs. He froze, looking back at the freezer and frowning in irritation. He worked hard on forcing himself to remember to feed her and the cunt didn't even appreciate it! He paused in front of the freezer, sneering at her stubby little fingers poking out from the lid.

Snatching one finger, he found himself surprised by how cold the little digit already was. Crunch. And now it was very broken. He bent it backward until the crunch of her knuckle reverberated against his palm. This minor act of aggression helped to release a fraction of that pent up rage that had been building. Her shriek was delightful. Somehow, she found the strength to rip her hand from where it was trapped so it could join her in the freezer.

He made his way upstairs, balancing everything as he left the screaming woman in the cold freezer.

His parents had insulated the basement and sound-proofed it so he could practice music while disturbing no one. They'd be stunned to learn how that gift benefited him now. At the top of the stairs, he dialed his code, which unlocked the heavy door. He did the wiring and built the device himself. It was definitely some of his better technical work.

The hinges pulled the door shut behind him. Thankfully, it happened a moment before a pale young woman appeared at his side wearing a big silly smile on her pout shaped pink lips. Her shimmering blue eyes lit up as they landed on him as she drew closer.

She threw long strands of dark brown hair over her shoulder before speaking. "I ate dinner."

He nodded, glancing at her from the corner of his eye while he tried to process what was happening. Her head tilted to her side, making her wavy hair practically flutter like silk as it adjusted to her movement. She pulled her bottom lip into her mouth and chewed it nervously as she waited for his response. Those beautiful, innocently wide eyes stared up at him through long, dark eyelashes.

Didn't he just-? Wasn't she in the-? He marched past her to enter the kitchen as he mentally questioned the current change in events. If his precious Anika was there, who was in the freezer? Maybe she wasn't there at all and he had actually put her in the-... NO. Anika was perfectly fine and following right behind him as he walked.

He looked down at the plates in his trembling hands, then to the sink base, where his little sister left her dirty dishes. Three sets? Oh yes. This was his proof that it definitely wasn't his Anika downstairs. He protected her by keeping her upstairs where she belonged. But, that begged the question, who did he put in the freezer, or was he imagining things?

It didn't take him long to wash all the dishes, the countertops, stove, and table where Anika had eaten alone. She stood next to the table, waiting silently while watching him. Feeling the need to entertain her, Slade turned to her and cocked an eyebrow.

"Did you do your homework?"

"Yes."

He began rinsing the cloth and called out to her over his shoulder.

"Clean your room?"

"Yes."

He hung the cloth up on the faucet and dried his hands on a tea towel. There was certainly more that she needed to do, but his mind was a foggy mess. His stomach turned, and he gave a sigh, finally thinking of another thing she needed to do.

"Take your vitamins?"

"My pills?" she blurted out with raised eyebrows before hurrying to the cupboard over the stove and opened it. "I'll do that now."

Going on her tippy toes to reach into the cupboard made her uniform skirt pull upward. He nearly flew into a rage at the thought of some boy at school seeing so high up the back of her legs. Slade swallowed the bile that rose in his throat as his lip peeled back.

"You need a bath tonight."

"Yep."

"Pardon?" His irritation over her improper response made his anger more obvious, though her quick response relieved some of the tension.

"Yes."

"Good girl."

Anika's skirt fluttered when she turned around. The troublesome girl gave him one of her mischievous grins as she walked to him. Her hand held out the child proof pill bottle up for him to open. He knew she could do it herself, but she always insisted on having him care for her. Always.

He easily opened the small bottle and scooped out her pill, using his index finger. He held the little pink pill out for her. Instead of taking it, she leaned forward and opened her mouth. Just like a child. Some things didn't change, no matter how old she got.

The damn girl was more adorable doing that than she had been when she was a child. Being a teenager made the action feel somewhat sexualized. Her moist tongue stuck out from between her rosebud lips as if wanting something in her mouth. Yes. She wanted her pill. Slade had to give himself a mental shake to calm down before he pressed the pill to her tongue. He waited patiently to watch the muscles in her throat flex to ensure she swallowed it.

"All done." She announced sweetly, fluttering those dark eyelashes at him.

"Good girl." They stood there, staring at one another for a moment before he spoke again. "It's bath night tonight."

"Right now?" She smiled and wrapped her thin arms around her torso, hugging herself.

"No, you can have ice cream and watch tv for half an hour, then bath."

"Yes."

Her responses were perfect. Exactly how he wanted them. She quickly turned and practically skipped her way into the living room like the carefree little creature he'd raised her to be. Her short uniform skirt fluttered behind her as a reminder of how he needed to behave himself. His dear sweet sister was an innocent trapped in this cage of a house with a monster like him.

His heart twinged in pain, remembering the cruel thing she said earlier that evening in her attempt to get attention from him. There was no way she could be pregnant. She worked and studied too hard to have the time to engage in something like that. He'd probably kill her if she did. Her desperate attempt to please him could be a radiant declaration of her love for him. Though it was likely that she could sense the darkness inside of him. Rightfully fearing it, she became too obedient. He hoped the former was true.

Slade frowned thoughtfully, though it twisted into a sneer as the obnoxious noise from the tv filled the open spaced living room. The show Anika turned on was some idiotic cartoon with anthropomorphic animals running around chasing one another. She wasn't allowed to watch anything else, though she was technically of age. He struggled to ensure her innocence and purity stayed intact. He needed to protect and shield her from everything in this horrific world. If he let technology melt her brain, she'd turn into the rest of those zombie-like idiot children. Today would be television after dinner and tomorrow he expected her to read a book. He was meticulous about everything in her life, ensuring balance for *everything.*

Turning toward the basement entrance, he made it two steps when a voice rang out in the nearby living room.

"Slade?"

"Yes?"

"What would you say if I wanted to call you daddy?"

Every fiber of his being halted, mentally cringing. *Daddy? What kind of question was that? Why would she even ask that? Did she want their parents back? Was he not sufficient for her?*

There was no point in answering. It was likely some sort of weird taunt. Anika could be expertly mischievous when she wanted to be. That girl was going to drive him beyond the brink of madness. Hell, she already was. Maybe she knew it.

The clueless girl was due for her bath and he needed to show restraint for a little while longer. How the fuck could he stop himself from giving in to his desperate desire to have her and take her body, destroying every bit of innocence she had?

That was who he left in the freezer... The only way he could restrain himself. His little replacement. Slade had his doll in the freezer. If she wasn't a figment of his imagination.

3

DISCOMFORT
Anika Darling

Anika watched as her beloved brother made his way out of view to go down to the basement. That was his favorite place. She hated that basement. frowned thoughtfully before a mischievous idea popped into her head. She turned to kneel on the couch with her elbows resting on the back of it.

"Can I call you Daddy?" she inquired, and waited for a response that didn't come.

She could see his reflection in the mirror next to the main entrance. Her precision timing ensured Slade would halt at the end of the hallway so she could witness his reaction. His features were harder to read than anyone else's. He made a dark, flat stare toward the living room, not knowing that she could see him. Anika toyed with her long hair.

Slade had always hated her father. She didn't blame him; the man was an absolute monster. Anika was only ten when their parents died, but she remembered the way they sat in their separate bubbles of space and embraced death, expecting their children to do the same. The amount of tranquilizer that they gave their kids should have ensured this, but for some miracle, it wasn't enough to keep either child unconscious. Her parents were arguing about how Daddy had been bad and would bring unwanted attention to the family. They eventually agreed that this was the only way. Anika faded in and out of consciousness until right before the water rose to meet the nose of the car.

The siblings were the only people who knew the truth behind their parent's 'accident'. When her mother drove off a bridge and into the water, she screamed in terror, waking her brother. The eighteen-year-old Slade pulled his sister from the rapidly sinking car and swam to safety, carrying her on his back.

The part that stood out the most for her from the entire memory was when Slade rushed back into the water to save one other thing. When she cried, the boy couldn't handle her tears and hurried back, not for their parents, but to save her doll.

Smirking to herself, she watched as the brother who raised her scuttled off to the basement. He spent a ridiculous amount of time locked away down there. He couldn't possibly still think that he was going to be a famous musician. Yet, he was constantly going downstairs, and she wasn't allowed to. There were times he went down, and she didn't see him for days.

With the door closed, she knew he would hear nothing from the main floor, so she was free to do anything she wanted. On one hand, she could just have her much deserved ice cream and watch the lame cartoon flickering obnoxious jokes across the screen, or she could find something else far more interesting to entertain herself. Rising to her feet, Anika stared around the living room with her bottom lip pulled into her mouth. She marched around the couch and then made her way down the hall. There was only one place in the house that could interest her.

Curiously, she stopped at the entrance to her brother's room. Slade left the door open as if inviting her in, but she knew he'd be livid to learn that she entered. The blackout curtains kept his room at an entirely different level of dark from the rest of the gloomy house. It took a moment for her eyes to adjust to the shadow. If she turned on his light, she feared he'd notice in some freaky way.

One foot. Then the other. Pushing his boundaries in little ways had become a game for her. The skin across her entire body prickled as she took a deep breath, taking in the scent of his room.

The combination of cleaning solution and cologne tickled her nostrils.

Slade meticulously placed everything in this little space. He was such a neat freak that she could lick the floor on any day, and it would taste like bleach. With a mischievous grin, she took a butterfly clip from her hair and slipped it beneath his pillow. Anika tugged on the corner of the pillow to adjust it, hoping to make it look the same as before she entered. There was still a possibility he'd notice the difference unless she distracted him until bedtime. Even pissed off, he'd never wake her up in the middle of the night. By the next day, his goldfish mind would forget anything that had upset him.

The corners of her lips pulled into a wider smile as she walked over to his precious computer. When he wasn't in the basement, this was where he sat. His work laptop rested closed in front of his computer monitor. To the right was a cute picture of them when they were children at the beach. She was a child and Slade was technically already a teen. He hadn't wanted to even be there, never mind to be forced to stand still, with his arms around his baby sister as picture proof of the family holiday.

She could barely remember that day. Aside from when he held her under the water. His face was expressionless, but so was hers. She simply laid there, waiting for him to let her up. He asked a few times over the years if she remembered the trip to the beach. She always said 'no'. Obviously, there was something he wished to talk about, but she'd never give him the chance to make peace with the memory. In Front of that framed picture was a cameo shot of her at her swim team meeting. Naturally, considering all her trauma around the water, she joined the swim club.

On the desk, next to his mouse, was a form with her school's logo and coat of arms scrawled across the top like some decadent banner. Anika Darling Graduation Registration Forms kept in plain sight to remind him to fill out for attendance and seating arrangements. *He registered for three seats. Was he going to make a show of being an orphan, just so he didn't have to sit directly next to anyone?* While lifting the paper to peek at the second page, she accidentally tapped the side of his mouse. His screen flashed on, blinding her momentarily.

Blinking back tears, she cocked her head to the side. His background was a cameo image of her from outside her bedroom window. She had her hands raised as she pulled a shirt over her head. The only garments on her slim body were her white panties and sports bra. It would have been a pushup bra if Slade would buy her some. But he insisted she wasn't developed enough.

With furrowed brows, Anika wondered if he actually went outside and took the picture without her knowledge when she would obediently allow him to take one.

The image pixelated for a moment and evolved into another one. The girl's locker room. Her teammates had been cropped out aside from the occasional arm or leg in the image's backdrop. She was naked, pulling on her swimsuit. How the fuck did he get that picture?!

Her heart thundered in her ears. Anika leaned forward with parted lips, panting light as if she would never get her breathing under control. Her hands cupped her breasts through her shirt, surprised at how they looked naked from such an angle. Is that what men found attractive? Or did these pictures hold the same sentiment as the ones he had displayed on the desk? She looked over at the two sitting on the desk's surface.

This had to be one of those things she just couldn't tell her friends about, or they'd loathe her brother. He was sweet and treated her like a little princess. Even though he was terrifying at the same time. There was just something about him that made people uncomfortable around him. She loved him so much and wanted to make him happy, too. He really was everything to her, and she owed him her life.

Trembling, Anika sat down in Slade's cushioned gaming chair. The picture on the monitor changed again to a candid of her in the bath. It was her backside, so no, her privates weren't visible. As if the one picture that didn't have her private parts in it was taken inside the house.

Her nipples suddenly became hard beneath her hands and extraordinarily sensitive. Testing her body's reaction, Anika lightly pinched her left nipple and twisted slightly, enjoying the peculiar tingle inside her breast. She could feel her sensitivity increase between her legs, making her clench her thighs tightly together.

She glanced over her shoulder toward the door, knowing her brother's temper would be completely unmanageable if he found her in his room. There were certain lines even she couldn't cross.

Her erect nipples bordered on painful when they pushed against the material of her bra. Her breaths were already rising and falling in harsh gasps as her arousal peaked.

Why did the thought of someone taking these sorts of pictures of her make her horny? She sat back in his chair and pulled her shirt up to expose her breasts. Anika whimpered softly when she pinched and lightly twisted her nipple.

The image changed to another candid, though that time it was taken in the change room at the swimming pool. Anika faced her locker with both arms lost inside as she dug for her clothes.

Her clitoris suddenly tingled so intensely that pee trickled out before she could stop it. Yelping loudly, Anika leaped to her feet and bolted from the room, leaving a trail of urine in her wake. Cupping her hands against her vagina did nothing to stop the liquid from gushing out.

By the time she reached the toilet, there was nothing left. Everything had trickled out, making a trail across the floor. FUUUUCK! If Slade came upstairs, she'd be so screwed!

Wasting no time, Anika quickly ripped off all her clothing and chuckled them into the laundry basket in the bathroom's corner, behind the door. She took a massive bundle of toilet paper and ran back to Slade's room, where she wiped down his chair. She cleaned her mess as best she could by dabbing it with the toilet paper. Cleaning, she made it way closer to the hallway.

If he came up from his little dank dungeon of a basement and found her in his room, it would be the end for her. Slade had a terrifying temper. She trembled at the thought of her brother catching her.

4

THE REPLACEMENT
Slade Darling

He pressed the buttons on the dial pad next to the basement door so the lock would click into place. What possessed her to ask him such a question?! The door shut behind him and he made his way down the stairs.

Was there even a girl in the freezer, or...

He used the key hanging on a nail next to the freezer to undo the lock. Flinging it open, he exposed the contents, unsure if he would find anything at all.

Bloody hands sprang forth from the opening, grabbing at the front of his shirt. The scream that followed was ear-piercing. Blood smeared from her fingertips onto the dark brown material. Several fingers were missing their nails from her desperate attempts to claw her way through the freezer's lid.

"Pweeve!" the girl begged.

Oh yes, he had a girl down here.

He had this doll for only a few weeks. The other day, she had the nerve to fight back and chomped down on his finger. So, he ripped out all her teeth in a white-hot flash of unbridled rage. Slade caught her icy wrists in his hands and gave her a shake to force her to look up at him.

"What do you have to say for yourself?" He snarled, glaring down at her terrified, puffy face.

It was rare for someone's touch to feel cold against his skin. He had poor circulation and always had cool extremities. He thoroughly enjoyed being the warm one, which played a part in his love of placing his dolls in the freezer for short periods of time.

"I'm forry! I woff you!"

Those words had him freeze in a peculiar combination of surprise and sudden arousal. Her wrists slipped from his fingers so her arms could wrap around the back of his neck in a desperate embrace. He could feel her pulling him downward toward her, or maybe she was trying to pull herself up.

"You love me?"

"I woff you! I woff you! I'm porry!"

Her entire body trembled and her breaths came in husky pants for air. As his arms wrapped comfortingly around her, he could feel her exhale against the side of his neck. Even that was cold. He moaned, knowing he didn't have much time, or *she'd* be up past her bedtime.

"Do you want me to warm you up?"

"YEFFF!"

He lifted her from the freezer. Her hands clutched tightly to his shirt, pressing it against his back. Her thin arms wrapped on either side of his neck, giving him chills, though he found he enjoyed the sensation of her face pressed into his throat more than any other part of her.

"Will you be a good girl now?"

"Yehh."

Her voice came out with a whimper into the crook of his neck. She physically trembled against him. He didn't have time to really play into his fantasy. The real one was waiting for him. His lips slowly curled into a smirk as he set her down on her little bare feet. She continued to hold her body pressed firmly against his, trying to absorb the small amount of body heat he created.

"You want to spend the night in the bed with blankets tonight, right? Instead of on the cold floor?

"Pweeb. I'm porry, puck me wip mo conbum."

She anxiously nodded, resembling a bobble head. She'd put that motion to good use shortly. The way she tried to show him it was acceptable for him to fuck her without protection when only a short while earlier she ruined his fantasy with her blubbering, annoyed him endlessly, but he was too horny to give a damn. His hands grabbed her upper arms to stop her movements, so he could stare deep into her eyes.

"Give me the best blowjob I've ever had, and I'll even give you extra blankets."

Her jaw quivered, but at least she didn't cry. He probably would have killed her if she started crying again. Or maybe he would have thrown her back in the freezer to cool her off again. He really didn't care if she lost fingers or toes like the last one. Eventually, he'd get bored with this doll, too.

"Yehhh."

She carefully lowered herself to her knees on the hard concrete floor. Her fingers fumbled with the front of his jogging pants as if they were difficult to remove. She pulled them down, exposing his limp cock to the chilly basement air. Her hesitation made him more excited as he anticipated the toothless warmth of her mouth.

This blow job was going to be painful for only one of them, and she deserved the pain after pissing him off so many times. He'd never forget the scream of terror she made when she woke up in agony, realizing he'd ripped out all her teeth. He smirked down at her, annoyed at how the swelling in her cheeks disfigured her once pretty face.

Her left hand encircled the shaft at the base as her other moved to his testicles. Her hands were like ice against his skin, but it caused no shrinkage in his bulky size. His cock had a wide girth and appeared stubby when soft, but as soon as the girl opened her mouth and the tip of her tongue touched his cock, the blood flow increased.

Her tongue was cool and wet as it swirled the helmet of his cock, before she pressed the tip to the small hole as if trying to massage it. He slowly cocked his head, watching curiously as her hands squeezed lightly, feebly massing. When he tripled in size, she turned her head, sticking her tongue out as far as she could, and rubbed it up and down the length. After a short while of her increasing the amount of slobber coating his dick, he frowned and cocked an eyebrow. It was as if she did everything she could to avoid having to actually suck his cock. He wanted suction power.

Instead of becoming aggressive or violent, he tenderly slipped his fingers into her matted hair. They pressed lightly against her scalp to maneuver her face so the tip of his cock could press against her lips.

Her eyes rolled back to stare up at him through long dark eyelashes as her lips parted slightly. It wasn't enough to fit his cock into her mouth. Her jaw quivered slightly, and those curvy eyebrows pulled inward, as if silently begging him not to make her do this. He pulled his hips away and moved forward so his dick tapped her mouth. She stopped massaging and simply sat there, holding his hard dick in her cool hands while pleading with her eyes for him not to fuck her face.

He applied more pressure to the tip of his dick against her mouth, so her lips would push against her gums. With a whimper, she opened her mouth, allowing him entry. That all-consuming fire encompassed his cock in a glorious embrace. Her tongue slithered up and down his length, but she didn't close her mouth around him and begin sucking. Shifting his hips, the top of his cock rubbed against the nub-like curve where her top set of teeth had once been. He almost moaned in pleased surprise from the heat radiating from the puckering, swollen wounds. He wiggled his hips, trying to encourage her to be more enthusiastic.

In a droll tone, Slade murmured, "I'm getting bored."

She still hadn't sucked, but at least more length entered her mouth as she allowed his tip to reach the back of her throat.

"You have three seconds to make this enjoyable for me."

She moved closer, pressing her forehead against his lower abdomen so the tip of his cock pulsed in the back of her throat. The constricting pleasure lasted moments before she gagged and pulled away. This was getting unbearably pathetic. Maybe ripping out her teeth for biting him had been a tad bit over-reactive.

With a sneer, he finally lost that fragmented smidge of patience and further tangled his fingers in the girl's hair. He gave her a hard shake to wake her up, before pulling her down until his cock pounded down her throat, suffocating her. She gagged, pushing against his thighs to free herself, but he ignored her, holding true. The more she struggled, the harder her throat constricted around him, making the sensation far more pleasurable. He felt her attempt to bite down, but only gummed his cock before attempting to shriek in pain. Air bubbles of oxygen bubbled out around his shaft, making her throat practically vibrate.

"Fucking dirty whore."

He slipped one hand under her chin to help anchor her head at the right angle. The real Anika was waiting for him, so he needed to hurry. The hand in her hair adjusted so he could press it against the back of her head and force her to move more aggressively.

"If I wanna fuck your ugly mouth, nasty piece of sh-."

With no more warning, he ripped her away from him. The horrid gagging sound as his swelled cock suctioned its way out of her throat was like music. She retched loudly, her tongue hanging out like the bitch she was. Slade grunted before ripping her forward, forcing his cock past her full lips and that gap where her teeth should have been. He mercilessly pounded himself into her mouth and down her throat, watching as tears rolled down her cheeks.

"-you better let me do whatever I fucking want, or I'll lock you in the freezer."

The fool girl wiggled, using her tongue to apply pressure to his cock. She breathed out so hard that snot bubbled out of her nostril, then dribbled from her nose. Her remaining fingernails dug into his thighs, and she suddenly clenched her jaw. Was she trying to bite him again? As if she hadn't learned her lesson the first time?! Her pocketed gums gnawed at his cock out of pure desperate terror.

He closed his eyes and forced himself to finish while holding her tight so she couldn't escape his juices. She gagged, choking and struggling. Her tongue rubbed the bottom of his length as if trying to push it out. Slade moaned, continuing to hold her as she wretched around his cock. When Slade finally released her, she fell backward, landing hard on the concrete. She coughed so hard that she had to roll onto her stomach, then hold herself up on her elbows. As if to irk him further, she retched loudly.

Slade snorted loudly before speaking, "you're pathetic."

Small bits of dinner that she consumed splattered from her mouth, landing on the floor. A white fiery rage built up, watching as her vomit ruined his clean floor. It was nasty concrete in the basement! The amount of work Slade put into keeping it immaculate was far too much for this dirty whore to mess with it.

His voice became dangerously low. "Clean it up," he snarled.

She floundered around, snatching her vomit up in her hands.

This thing had become a revolting creature.

"You are boring me," Slade whispered in a flat tone of voice.

He turned and marched toward the stairs, unable to bear looking at the decrepit little creature any longer. He didn't even bother to chain her up, using the manacles he attached to the cement floor near the four corners. He just wanted to get the fuck away from the nasty thing and go help his sister.

His slipper-covered feet stomped on each wooden step, making the loud thunk echo in the dank space. He felt completely dissatisfied with this version of his dear sister. She was a revolting disappointment. He pressed the code for the door while he considered what he was going to do about the nasty creature crying on the floor below.

Slade ripped the door open and stepped into the hallway. He nearly walked toward the kitchen, where the sound and light from the tv called him, when a gut feeling drew him in the opposite direction.

Slowly, Slade's head swiveled to turn his gaze down the dark hallway. A bright glow streamed into the confined space from the bathroom, lighting up the young woman on her hands and knees as she frantically scrubbed the floor with a massive wad of toilet paper. His brows drew down curiously.

She froze. Her face turned to stare up at him with a look of surprise and horror. Her tanned cheeks turned rosy as her mouth hung open for a moment before she

"I peed my pants!"

He cocked an eyebrow, suddenly realizing she was not wearing a single stitch of clothing. Why was she naked? Making a growl in the back of his throat, he stomped up the hall toward the silly girl. Slade had to take a moment and give a loud sigh while he struggled to find his inner calm. He grabbed the handle of the closet door midway down the hall.

"Go run your bath water." It was a serious struggle not to admire her naked body as he spoke to her.

His voice was flat and emotionless in his command. She knew better than to get into the bath without his presence, so there was nothing to worry about. He got to the sink and placed the bucket in it before running hot water. He squirted some soap into the bucket while watching the water rise. Once it was half full, he carried the bucket and mop down the hall. He started at the end of the hall and moped straight down, stopping when he reached the area Anika was scrubbing. He looked into the bathroom where the trail led and frowned thoughtfully while examining her expressionless face. She was up to something mischievous again. That deviant child was always doing things to drive him crazy.

He continued mopping and froze, realizing how wrong something felt. His monitor was on. That meant someone had touched his mouse. The room was lit up by a picture of Anika sleeping naked on her bed with her sheets in a ball at the bottom corner of her bed. She laid spread eagle, so her entire world was visible through the lens of his camera.

"You were in my room." His voice came out dangerously low as he pulled the door shut to block her view of his monitor.

"I wanted my graduation forms." She pouted, with her big innocent blue eyes, cluelessly staring up at him. "I was scared you'd miss it, but you aren't done filling them out."

"Have I ever missed anything important to you?"

"No, but..."

"But?" he switched hands with the mop and gave her a dark look while shifting his weight onto his heels.

"You don't spend time with me anymore. I miss you."

As Anika spoke, her shoulders hunched so her arms could easily wrap around her torso, pinching her tiny breasts together. Her knees pulled tightly against one another, and her toes curled. She tilted her head forward and cocked it to the side so she was looking up at him through her long, sandy blonde eyelashes. Everything about her body screamed that she was desperate for attention.

Slade sighed, dropping a hand to his side before speaking. "We live together. We see each other every day. I provide for you, and your needs are met in every way." By the end of his explanation, he was feeling as hopeless as his dear sister looked.

"Not in every way. I need attention."

He snorted, "Of course you do."

He gave her a slightly smirk though, his eyes narrowed as he felt compelled to stare at his bedroom floor for a moment. He shook his head slowly as another thought occurred to him.

She probably pissed on his floor.

"You're growing older. You won't need or want me around soon." He reminded her of his own greatest fear for the umpteenth time.

He continued mopping his way down the hall as Anika clapped back.

"I love you, Slade. You're my perfect big brother. I love you more than anything."

His hand curled around the bucket's handle as his eyes moved from the clear water to her face. She was so sincere in her declarations of love, but he knew better. She deserved more than this decrepit monster before her. Slowly, he shook his head before turning his back and walking toward the kitchen, carrying his bucket and mop.

While pouring the water down the drain, he was unsurprised to find the water clean. He washed his floors constantly. He would lose track of the days and probably washed them multiple times a day just to make sure that everything remained perfectly maintained. He rinsed the bucket out and even washed the mop thoroughly before returning them to the closet on his way back to Anika.

Coming into the bathroom, he froze, admiring the glorious view before him.

Still naked, Anika was bent over the side of the massive cast iron tub. Her perfect, perky little ass was facing the entrance as he walked in. This was his own personal torture. How could she innocently not know how insane she drove him? Every small curve of her body seemed designed to drive him crazy with a lust that could never be satiated. Anika leaned forward to check her water temperature. The way she bent over so flexibly far pulled her small ass cheeks apart so he could see her tight little asshole beckoning to him. Just beneath that tasty pink hole were her two delicious plump-looking pussy lips pinched together by her thighs.

"Slade?" she whispered, turning just her head to face him as he sat down on the toilet lid with his eyes drawn to her bottom.

He attempted to hide his raging hard-on as he supervised her.

"Hmm?" he purred his response, forcing his gaze to shift to meet hers.

"I think it's too hot. Can you check?"

It felt as though all the air was sucked from the room. He brought a hand up and covered his mouth, letting his fingers drag down the stubble of his chin hairs.

He had no choice. Slade stood up and walked over to the side of the tub, ignoring his massive cock as it bounced excitedly off the soft material of his sweatpants. He should start wearing boxers. It might help to keep the damn thing at bay. Every step made his thundering bulge more noticeable.

He stood in front of her, staring down into those stunning deep blue eyes for a moment before turning and bending over to touch the water. His fingers slipped beneath the surface to test it for her. It was lukewarm, almost cold, but that was how she liked it. Slade needed the water to feel like it could burn his skin for him to enjoy it.

"It feels fine." He murmured, leaning further to slip his entire forearm beneath the surface, just in case he was wrong.

"Is it?" Anika lifted a leg over the side of the tub and hesitantly dipped her toes in.

Noticing her foot next to him, he trailed his eyes up her leg. At that angle, she exposed the pink center of her most delicious area to him with her lips parted, drawn by her spread thighs. It took everything in him not to stare directly at her pussy and force his gaze to move to her navel. His greatest fear was that he would lose the small fragments of self-control he had and take her body.

He licked his lips and clenched his jaw before taking a long breath. Breathing to find calm was a therapy technique he'd learned when the siblings were ordered by the state to do therapy after their parents' deaths. It was a part of the mandate for him to receive custody of Anika. This time, however, the feeling he had was anything but calming. The smell of her was faint and masked by chlorine from her extra-curricular activities. The only thing he could smell with the moist, sweet, earth tones of her pussy. His eyes shifted back to the location that mouthwatering essence permeated from.

Her hand moved to Slade's shoulder to help keep her balanced as she carefully entered the tub. He could feel her icy hand through his shirt, giving him chills. She was the only person in the world whose flesh felt cold to him without needing to be put in a freezer. Her touch was amazing to him. Even the most innocent of caresses sent waves of bliss across his body.

"Thank you."

Anika's smile was warm and sweet. She stared down at him, making him very conscious of every small move he made. He was a grown man and somehow became completely mesmerized by her every movement, so much so that he was frozen with his hand still in the water. With one of her hands already resting on his shoulder, she moved the other to the top of his head. Those thin, nimble fingers toyed with his silky dark hair, cooling his feverish skin with the slightest of touches.

This time, he couldn't help but look straight ahead at her beckoning pussy. The little wisps of hair announced her presence in adulthood. His mouth watered enough that he had to swallow, which brought him back to reality. This was *not* one of his dolls.

She was Anika, the untouchable one.

5

SWEET BROTHER
Anika Darling

The tepid water felt so soothing as it swished between her toes, making her skin tingle. She wiggled them, basking in the warmth and blood flow it brought to the little digits.

Nearly losing her balance, Anika placed a hand on her brother's shoulder to make sure she didn't fall as she clumsily climbed into the tub. She turned her body toward him and placed her other foot on the edge of the tub, scared to put it in the water in case it was too warm for that one. Her circulation was awful, which made the warm water reach different levels of painful for each limb. She pulled her elbows in tight to her sides, pressing into her ribs as goosebumps rose across her skin. The motion brought her small breasts toward the center of her chest, by squishing them together. The cool air made her nipples become painfully hard.

Deciding it was time to put her other foot in the water, she reached forward to rest her other hand on Slade's head. His hair was so soft and nice to touch. He wasn't ever greasy or gross like the boys her own age, and he always smelled so good. As far as she was concerned, her brother was the kindest and sweetest person in the world.

He fell for her 'it's too hot' routine every day, just so she could have more attention from him. Maybe he liked simply taking care of her in whatever way he could. She moved her fingers, allowing his hair to slip between them. His skin felt feverishly warm to her icy fingertips.

"Thank you, Slade."

Her voice shook when she watched his eyes slowly trailed up her naked form to look at her face. In a moment of surprise, she brought her eyebrows to the center, furrowing them out of concern. She moved her fingers from the top of his head down to the slight bump and scratch above his left eye. *Had that been there the previous day?*

After reading her expression, his gaze moved back down her body as if in search of any wounds on her. She took meticulous care of herself, knowing he'd find the slightest bump or scratch and absolutely lose his shit over it. It was obvious because he cared so deeply for her.

With both feet in the water, she balanced on her heels and wiggled her toes. Anika slid one of her legs forward until it bumped into the back of his hand, which he seemed to have forgotten in the water. She smiled down at him as his eyes met hers. Maybe he would read with her later... but she knew it was a false hope. He'd disappear into his precious basement, and she knew it. She was lucky he took the time to let her have a bath instead of making her take a shower so he wouldn't have to keep guard over her.

"Please wash yourself quickly. It's almost bedtime."

After a moment's pause with the back of his hand touching her shin, he moved a safe distance away to sit on the toilet and observed her. She felt as if she could suddenly breathe again without him so close. What was wrong with her? Why was she always so focused on doing things to pick on and antagonize her brother? If he lost his temper, things could get very dangerous, quickly. She looked over at his face and felt an inkling of fear when she saw that false smile tugging at the corners of his lips, as if he were already suppressing his anger.

It was best if she simply did as she was told. She turned her back on Slade and bent over to turn off the faucets. The tub wasn't even half full, but the higher the water level got, the more anxious her dear brother would become. There was a time and place to put him on edge, and if she pissed him off in the wrong way while he seemed so out of it, he could lose control completely. The thought had her pursing her lips while trying to shake off the anxiety that built. He would never hurt her on purpose.

The water swished around her, sloshing up and down on the sides of the tub as she carefully sat. Anika shivered, her jaw quivering as the water rose around her, displaced by her presence. She laid down in the tub with only her knees, breasts and face poking out from the surface. Her hair fluttered around her like jellyfish tentacles. She loved the feel of water, and the way it hugged every curve and crevasse. A slight smile taunted her lips as she waited for the inevitable.

There he was. Slade could no longer handle being unable to see her while knowing she was in the water. He stood to check on her and make sure she wasn't drowning. With his eyes on her, she raised her eyebrows before sitting up, pretending as if she hadn't lingered out of sight on purpose to make him uneasy.

With water trickling down her long hair, and rolling across her skin, she pulled her hair over her shoulder and squeezed it lightly to ring out some of the water. She whimpered softly, realizing how sore her upper arms were from her training. Her blue eyes darted around the water's surface in search of her soaps. That gaze shifted to her brother's face with a pleading expression.

"I forgot my stuff..."

Her pout was fake, but he obeyed the wordless demand, anyway. Slade marched across the narrow room, making small gusts of wind in his wake. Anika shivered as the cool air tickled her skin, hardening her nipples and making gooseflesh rise across her arms and back.

He bent over in front of the sink, giving her the opportunity to admire his plump bottom. Why did he have a nicer ass than her? He took out her plastic basket, which contained the four bottles of soaps for her to use.

He frowned into the basket and approached the side of the tub.

"It feels a little light." He muttered before placing the floating basket on the water's surface above her feet. "Add them to the list on the fridge if you want any replaced."

"Okay, thank you, Slade!" She tried to sound excited to lighten the mood, which felt almost threatening.

It almost felt as if there was a presence in the air of some unseen force warning her to be careful. Nervously, she swallowed and leaned forward to pick up the bottle of face wash. The plastic felt cold against her warmed skin. Anika applied it to her skin, massaging in slow clockwise circles to deepen its effect. She left it on her face to give it time to soak into her pores. Replacing the bottle into the basket, she picked up the shampoo next. Her eyes shifted to her brother's face as she squirted some onto her palm. She gave him a friendly smile while she lathered the shampoo between her hands. She was very conscious of her brother's protective gaze. His eyes practically made her skin prickle now that she was raising her hands above her head.

Thoughts of those naked pictures on his monitor suddenly made her face feel like it was on fire. Would that sort of discovery change anything between them? Was she still just his sweet little sister? Her heart thundered in her ears as her hands massaged her scalp. Her small breasts barely moved from her shift in positions, though she wished they had more of a woman's circumference than a young girl's. She was a grown woman. Normally, she would massage her scalp longer, but her arms throbbed painfully.

She laid back down and rinsed her hair, this time allowing her face to go beneath the surface. Her hands scrubbed quickly to rinse the soaps from her face and scalp before she sat up, gasping for air. Again, he had stood next to the tub to ensure she would rise above the surface.

When she rose from the water, he sat back down. Maybe watching their parents drown had traumatized him more than it did her. They had always been distant and were never home. With her brother continuing to take care of her, it was as though nothing had changed from before they died.

Taking a little longer to apply conditioner, she massaged it into her scalp, closing her eyes and enjoying the sensation until she had an idea. Her hands fell to her sides, and she turned to face her brother with a pout.

"Can you wash me? My arms are tired."

His flat stare said it all. Nope. Not happening.

It had been months since he last agreed to wash her. What changed in those months? Her mouth tightened into a knot before her blue eyes narrowed malevolently. Maybe she was a little spiteful. She was a swimmer on the swim team and had beautiful muscle definition in her arms and should be able to handle such a simple task as washing herself. However, he was supposed to take care of her and lately, he'd been slacking.

The water rippled around her as she finished massaging her scalp and slid her hands along the long tendrils of pale blond hair to ensure maximum coverage. She moaned softly when her hands returned to massage her scalp a little more. It felt so good! Nearly every day she wore a swim cap and rubbing her head was the biggest relief of pressure for her.

The tension in her arms had already become unbearable and she let her hands drop into the water. She was lifting weights at the gym that week during her lunch hour, and her arms really were a little sore. Not as sore as she made them out to be. She gave her brother a side-eye glance.

He sat on the toilet lid with his legs crossed and an elbow resting on his knee with his chin in the palm. He looked so bored.

Anika laid down in the water, annoyed by how quickly it had turned outright cold. She put her head back so the water could soak her scalp, but after a few moments, an idea came to her.

With a playful grin painting her lips, Anika waited in that position a little while longer. When she was sure Slade was about to check on her, she held her breath and slipped her face beneath the surface until the back of her touched the base of the tub. She blinked, feeling the water tickle her eyeballs. Any moment, he would poke his head over the side of the tub to check on her.

Mischievously, she grinned to herself.

There he was. Her knight in shining armor, glaring down at her in more than just mild irritation. *No.* She needed to hold true to her path because if she gave in now, this would never work again. She let a bubble of air slip from her nose as they made eye contact. He crossed his arms over his chest and cocked an eyebrow at her. The thing he might not realize was that because of the swim team, she could hold her breath for a ridiculous amount of time. It was a matter of if his will would break before she fainted from lack of oxygen and actually drowned.

Expecting him to reach into the water and pull her up, she felt mildly disappointed when he moved toward the other end of the tub and disappeared from her sight. That bastard was calling her bluff. Maybe she really should just let herself drown to prove her point.

An icy hand grabbed her ankle and lifted her leg from the water, startling the shit out of her. Anika gasped and then choked. She sat up onto her elbows, coughing hard from the water that made its way into her lungs. She glared at her brother, who leaned over the side of the tub with her ankle in one hand and a soapy cloth in the other.

Water dribbled down the sides of her face and into her eyes from her hair as she tried her most menacing glare at the man. He looked far too pleased with himself, even though none of his features changed in the slightest. Cocking an eyebrow, he lightly dragged the cloth along the bottom of her foot, making her twitch. She gasped and flinched away as he moved his hand up and down.

He quickly caught her foot in an iron tight grip that bordered on painful. Slade stuck out one finger with the cloth covering it and slipped it between her big toe and the one next to it. The ticklishness bordered on agonizing when he twisted his hand back and forth with that damn finger between her toes. The next gap was way worse and practically sent sensations tippling across her foot and up her leg. That time, she pulled free from his grasp and dropped her limb back into the water.

That was when her naughty brother smirked, showing his merciless side, "Come now, you want me to wash you, don't you?"

"But it tickles!" she pouted, "and you're taking too long there on purpose!"

"I noticed you barely wash between your toes. You're going to end up with some sort of rash." He cocked his head to the side and added in a soft, threatening voice. "That's not the only ticklish place on your body. Are you sure you want me to wash you?"

She growled audibly through grit teeth before raising her foot and placing her ankle back in his hand. She was going to accept this torture just to get what she wanted. He would wash her, spoiling her like he used to when she was little. However, the way his eyes moved up her body to her face, then back down to her foot, didn't feel the same as when she was younger. Something changed in their dynamic, but she did not know what that meant for their relationship.

She giggled, bringing her wet hands to her mouth to stifle it and hide her reaction. The water dripped on her breasts from her forearms, giving her chills as they trickled down the sides of the small humps. Her nipples became hard as she fought not to squirm beneath his touch. She couldn't wait for him to move on and wash her breasts. For some weird reason, she liked touching them so much. Just the thought of her nipples being pinched made her aroused, but it wasn't enough to distract her from her brother's devious touching.

"Slade! I can't!" she whimpered. "It tickles!"

She curled her toes, trying to make it more difficult for him, but he forced his way into the tight space without remorse. Her other foot planted onto the bottom of the tub as she lifted her midsection from the water. It took every bit of inner strength not to pull away.

"Ow. It hurts. Be gentle."

His finger moved down from the crevasse it had violated, following the curve along the underside of her toes to the next waiting entrance. His touch became gentler, which only worsened the sensation. Her abdomen clenched. She quivered before obnoxiously gasping and ripping her foot from his grasp.

"Not that gentle!" Anika yelled at him.

Her own voice echoed loudly off the hollow bathroom walls, startling her. Luckily, her yell didn't upset him. Instead, the damn fool looked more pleased than anything.

"Come back here." His voice was a tender purr unlike anything she'd ever heard from her dear brother.

With a pout she responded, "I have to pee, though."

Anika pressed her thighs together as if in evidence. She really felt as if she needed to pee. It wasn't as bad as when she was in his room, but the sensation of building pressure was definitely climbing with every moment he spent tickling her foot.

Looking so forlorn, she couldn't help but obey his request, he whispered, "I'm not finished with you."

With her lips parted, she pried her legs apart before delicately returning her foot to his cool hands. He dragged the cloth along the ridge under her toes, watching as she trembled, while trying not to pull away again.

Anika whimpered softly, stifling a laugh before masking a quiet giggle with a moan. Her hands came up and covered her face, splashing water across her abdomen and breasts. She pressed them to her skin before parting her fingers to peek down at her brother, who had a gleam in his eye as he watched her reactions.

"It's too much. Please, just get it over with. I can't handle this."

Her begging seemed to fall upon deaf ears.

Slade replied, crinkling his nose, "I need something to make it slide better. When you squeeze it closed like that, I can't get in there."

He reached down into her floating basket and grabbed the bottle of liquid soap. Slade rinsed the cloth again before sitting up and grinning down at her. He turned to sit on the edge of the tub, not releasing her foot. Carefully, her older brother lifted her foot more, parting her thighs to place her foot on his thigh. The movement made her very conscious of her pussy as the lips pulled apart and the cooling water licked at the sensitive flesh.

She whimpered quietly before she could stop herself. He was smirking at her. A genuine little smile tugged at the corners of his lips, making her face drain of color. Her heart thudded wildly in her chest, making her breath come in wheezing gasps. *Why was she so scared of such an expression?*

He squeezed the cold soap from the container directly onto her toes, coating them with the slimy goop. Anika gasped and curled her toes, feeling the ickiness spread down her foot. He watched it spread and appeared to be enjoying the wait as it oozed down her skin.

When it nearly reached her heel Slade used the cloth to catch it, soaking his pant leg. He used the cloth to massage her foot. After a few more minutes of making her squirm and whimper, he started washing his way up her calf and shin, ensuring the bubbles spread sparingly. He stopped at her knee and held his hand out.

"Other foot."

Her stomach fluttered and head spun. "You didn't finish that leg." Her desire for him to wash her thigh next felt strangely overwhelming.

He gave her a flat stare, tilting his head forward and staring with narrowed eyes. His cheeks seemed to redden, potentially from anger. She really was a little too bossy for her own good.

In order to soothe him, she added a single word, "Please."

She inched down the tub so her wet, soapy calf could rest across his thigh. The movement pulled her legs further apart, though the uncomfortable position wasn't an issue if he actually finished washing her. His eyes trailed down her body, from her face, to her breasts, navel and below until they landed on her thigh. He took the cloth and slid it down the back of her thigh.

His breathing was coming in sharp gasps, as if he had run a great distance. Up her thigh, then down. She focused on not flinching when he reached the extremely sensitive flesh of her upper thigh.

Slade leaned forward so that he could wash the back of her thigh. He broke the surface of the water so his fingertips, covered by the cloth, could slide over her bottom. His touch was barely present in the movement and it vanished entirely once the side of his hand touched the tub's base. Anika nearly sighed in relief when his hand slid back up her leg to the back of her knee. It returned quickly, and this time, his cloth covered fingers slid between her ass cheeks.

She focused on not reacting, as if she didn't even notice how sensitive the spot he touched was. Her stomach dropped, and she nearly peed. Then the sensation was gone when he returned the sopping wet cloth to the surface.

He brought the cloth to her knee and slid it back down her inner thigh. He nearly touched her pussy, but pulled away. She whimpered and flinched when the cloth slipped from his grip and the corner touched the lips of the area that he seemed so keen to avoid.

At that, he twitched violently and dropped her leg back into the water. He stood, glaring down at her like he was coming to his senses or something.

"You're done." He snapped.

Slowly she shook her head, forcing a pout on her full lips, "I'm not."

While yanking out the plug, Slade turned on the water and set it to shower. Anika screamed in surprise as cool water exploded from the shower head, splattering across her body. She sat up, coughing and using her forearm to protect her face.

"No more bath, just finish washing up and get ready for bed."

"But-."

Anika's mouth hung open as she watched her brother bolt from the room. He didn't even close the shower curtain. Did he feel the need to run away from the idea of spending time with her because he was so revolted by her, he couldn't stand it?

The cold water slowly turned lukewarm as she sat there shivering beneath the torrent. The surface quickly lowered as the drain expelled the liquid from the tub twice as fast as the faucet filled it. Anika barely noticed the tub emptying while she sat there. It took a few minutes before she could shake herself from her zoning out.

Anika quickly washed herself while grumbling quietly to herself. She was finally getting some attention from him, and then he left. Damn jerk.

6

DIABOLIC SISTER
Slade Darling

The moment he escaped from the bathroom, his thundering heart slowed its rhythm. His pulse raced so hard that his head spun and his vision blurred. She was the only thing in the world that could make him feel anything real.

Behind his closed eyes, he could still see her naked frame swallowed up by that shimmering water as she parted her legs like she wanted him, too. No. He could never do that to her. She wasn't one of his dolls. That was Anika. His beautiful and truly sweet little sister was innocent in all of this.

Leaning back against his bedroom door, which he didn't even remember closing, he waited for his body to get under control. The heart palpitations slowed, but his massive erection had yet to wane. Shaking his head, Slade took several steps into his room before freezing.

He sniffed the air, detecting something out of the ordinary floating up from beneath the mixed scents of his cologne, air freshener spray and bleach. His ridiculous sense of smell was why he kept meticulous care of his home.

It was possible his suspicion was correct and Anika had pissed in his room. He wanted so badly for her to pee in the tub when he was tickling her. The last time something like that happened was about six months previous when they were wrestling. She had him 'pinned' beneath her when he started tickling her sides. The girl had no control over that. She pissed all over his chest. Her humiliation over the incident was enough that he came in his pants and even with his loathing of all things dirty, it took him weeks before he could force himself to wash the urine from that sweater, which he'd kept in a bag hidden at the back of his closet. It was simply something in knowing that it came from her body that drove him wild. It was shortly after that when he realized his feelings regarding his step sister had changed. He was smart, incredibly so, but exceptionally socially awkward.

He squatted, sniffing again. The faintest of smells tickled his nose. His hands pressed onto the wood floor as he brought his face closer, before closing his eyes and breathing deep. The sweet and tangy smell of her urine seemed smeared across the floorboards. His cock throbbed painfully inside his sweats, as if desperate for attention. The head of the engorged mass was practically tingling in anticipation.

There was no holding back. Slade shifted his pants to expose his dick and took destiny into his own hand. He eased himself down onto the floor, partially laying on his side so he could press his forehead into the wood grain, while his other hand could masterfully work the length of his dick. With every breath, he could practically taste her. He closed his eyes tightly to visualize the way it appeared when her legs parted and that delectable little pearl of sensation and desire became visible. His fingers tightened around his thick shaft and with every motion he vividly fantasized about penetrating that small hole. Each inhale only made that scenario feel more real as his pulsating cock quickly breached its climax. A little too quickly.

Slade shifted his supporting arm so he could bite down on his wrist and mute his moan as he came closer to finishing. Furrowing his eyebrows, Slade gasped loudly against his skin as he finally came. His cum spilled forth, dribbling across his fingertips and splattering the floor atop Anika's smeared piss. He took one more deep breath before rolling onto his back and letting his dick lull over the waistband of his pants.

He couldn't even bother to peel himself up from the floor. The minutes ticked by with him enjoying the afterglow of cumming until he heard the shower click off. Hearing her rummaging around in the bathroom brought back the mental image of her naked, wet body.

He needed to go get her ready for bed by making sure she flossed and brushed her teeth. But he really didn't want to move away from this moment in time.

Taking care of his sister was his responsibility. When he was sixteen, on the day he tried to drown her, he promised himself he would let nothing bad happen to her again. So far, he's done his utmost to ensure that. The girl was wearing his self-control, though.

Every word she whimpered, everything she said in that bathroom. The way her pussy looked beneath that glittering surface seemed to drive his hormones into oblivion. His heart raced again as blood thundered down the length of his cock, making him impossibly hard once more. Why?! What the fuck!? This was what he had dolls for! Using them was supposed to be a way of preventing this from happening around her!

There was a timid knock at his door before a voice followed. "Slade, I need my kiss and hug goodnight."

Damit!

"I can come tuck you into bed in a minute," he growled, quickly standing up and slipping his cock back into his pants.

There was no hiding it!

Normally, he could be so much more careful about controlling himself, but the past few days, that doll downstairs had been a poor substitute for what he really wanted. The last several days, he'd practically had non-stop boners that seemed to return no matter what he did.

"What if you forget again?..." her voice was so pitiful. "Did you stop loving me?"

That question burned a fiery rage in him. Slade snatched the door handle with his cum soaked hand and reefed the door open, exposing his precious sister. His gaze darted to her pretty blue eyes, but immediately became drawn to something else.

"Uh- where are your pajamas?"

She tilted her head to the side. Water rolled off her hair and trickled down her naked body. Her arms and legs had goosebumps and her nipples were so deliciously hard.

His breath caught in his throat as he found himself unable to pry his gaze from a particular droplet of water that seemed gloriously adventurous as it traveled the terrain of her small body. With a dry mouth, he swallowed, but there was nothing there to push down.

"I forgot them in my room. I already brushed my teeth, so I thought I'd save myself from backtracking and get my kiss and hug now, then just get dressed and go straight to bed after."

She was naked.

"I-uh. Did you floss?"

And wet.

"Yup."

And cold.

"Hmm?" He honestly hadn't heard her response.

"Uh- yes," she corrected herself before raising her arms and holding them out toward him in search of a hug.

There was no way she wasn't going to feel his cock, swollen and pressing against the front of his jogging pants. However, the longer he stared at her with that sad, yet hopeful expression, the more painfully his heart palpated. *Fine.*

"Come."

He reached out with his free hand to invite her into his embrace. She moved in, practically slamming her cold, wet body against his. He was used to hugging her after swimming, when her skin was like ice, but knowing she was entirely naked, pressing herself against him made blood rage into his cock. She pressed her face against his throat as he bowed his head.

He pried his other hand from its cum-filled grip on his door handle to wrap that arm around her naked form. He balled it into a fist, so he didn't accidentally wipe his juices on her. Through the thin material of his shirt, he could feel her hard nipples, making him wish he, too, wasn't wearing anything at all. The thought was too much for him, combined with the fact that her hands moved to the sides of his face and pulled his lips down to meet hers in a gentle kiss. The sensation nearly made him swoon.

He almost moaned into her mouth as he climaxed, soaking the front of his gray sweatpants. It left a dark mark that spread before trickling down his pant leg.

She gasped, pulling away. "You peed your pants, too." She giggled. "We are definitely family."

Her playful laugh only made him more swollen. It was as if he could never get rid of it. She slipped her hand into his and led him out of his room and toward the bathroom before he could argue. He was extremely insecure about the fact that the hand she so securely clutched onto still had semi-dried cum all over it.

As they walked, she looked over her shoulder while speaking to him, "We better get you taken care of. Just like you take care of me."

He slightly waddled, using his free hand to pinch the moist material to keep the cold wetness from rubbing his already insanely sensitive cock.

"You need a bath."

He never bathed. Only showered. He hated the feeling of the water hugging all around him, suffocating him. He sneered as his eyes flashed to glare at the massive bathtub while she moved closer to it and turned on the faucets. Anika pulled the nub to plug it before turning to him with a playful grin.

"Don't be like that! It's the only way I can help you get cleaned up."

His teeth grit and he shook his head. He really could take care of it himself and as he opened his mouth to say that very thing, she slid to her knees in front of him. The words seemed lost and his mind fumbled to remember exactly how to function. Her icy fingers slipped into the waistband over his hips and yanked his pants straight down to his ankles in one swift motion.

What the fuck was he supposed to do now?! The sudden release freed his throbbing cock from its cotton prison. The rock-hard mass bound happily from the waistband, and smacked the girl on her face.

The pair both gasped, and he prepared for her to freak out as any woman in their right mind would. At least, the women he'd been with had. That joke was in poor taste, considering most of the women he'd enjoyed were his dolls.

"Wow! It's so big!" she announced, catching it in a tight grip. "Look how huge it is beside my hand!" she slid her hand up and down the length as if emphasizing its mass. "Oh, it's still dirty inside. Look."

She rubbed her thumb over the tip, causing shock waves of

sensation to radiate across his entire body. As she moved the finger in circles over the opening, small amounts of white beaded out and dripped down, trickled onto her cheek. She didn't even seem to notice as it moved like a tear down her face before dripping from her chin.

"Anika." Slade's own voice surprised him by coming out in a desperate whimper.

"Look at it. I wanna get it out."

With no more warning, her mouth engulfed his cock in a flaming vortex of unadulterated pleasure. A horrific and guttural sound of pleasure and terror erupted from deep in his chest. He physically trembled. Having blown his load twice was already too much and far more than he was normally capable of. A third time was bound to border in agony. Her tongue pushed its way out of her mouth, applying the perfect amount of pressure underneath. It hung out past her lips and massaged the place where his rod and balls met.

"Fuck." His hands curled around the back of her head, toying with her cold, wet hair. "Oh, I love you."

The pain in his chest was nearly unbearable. There was a tingling across his body, which became a numb throbbing in his hands and feet.

She practically swallowed his cock with masterful practice. He wasn't ready for it to be over yet, but Anika pulled away. Slade felt he had no choice but to allow her to do as she wished.

"Bathe with me," she encouraged.

His anxiety heightened as his eyes darted briefly toward the tub as he shook his head. "I don't want to."

Her cool hands slid up the sides of his hips beneath his shirt, making goosebumps rise on his skin. They brought his shirt upward with them as they tickled his ribs. Slade basked in her icy touch, feeling her press her body against his while she pushed the shirt up over his head. Her cold flesh stressed every small curve, making his skin feel all that much more feverish. Her small breasts pressed against the place on his stomach between his ribs, though he wished they were laying down so they could be against his chest. His hands trembled when the thought of moving them to her waist occurred to him.

When she spoke, her hot breath caressed his chest. "Do you want more?"

Her tongue flicked out, licking his nipple. Slade couldn't help flinching in surprise. No matter how badly he wanted it, the thought of going in that tub filled with water made him feel sick. She stepped away, as if for emphasis.

"Fuck." He groaned, feeling a dull ache in his chest.

He stumbled forward on weak legs. The closer he got to the pooling water, the deeper the tub looked. It was full enough, but when he reached to shut off the water, she moved to block the faucet by placing one foot in the tub. Liquid still rolled down her body from her hair, streaming along every crease. He watched as the perfect pearl of water rolled down between her breasts, past her navel and to the divide in her pussy lips. He wanted so badly to taste where the droplet so greedily wandered.

Gathering up his courage, Slade also lifted a foot and dipped it into the water. It wasn't so bad. It was warm, thankfully. He allowed himself one more deep breath before climbing into the tub and sitting down. Like ripping off a band aide, he plopped down hard onto his ass, with the water sloshing around him. It was difficult not to shake, but he didn't want to seem like a wimp in front of his sister. Not so bad... was it?

His cock was masterfully erect, as if knowing exactly what was to come.

"Good boy." His sister teased before stepping the rest of the way into the rising water. "You're always so good, taking such care of me. Please. Slade, take care of me a little more."

As she spoke, she walked closer to him, sliding her feet along the bottom of the tub on both sides of his legs. She drew closer until her hands could tangle in his hair. She pulled his face closer to her body. He parted his lips, prepared to accept her upon his tongue when she suddenly sat down. Her knees gave way, and she flung downward until their bodies collided, halted her collapse.

His cock slipped into her virgin entrance far too easily and with no pain. He'd had virgins before, and they all complained about the pain at first. His eyes moved to the water, which hadn't turned red, but appeared cloudy. The inability to see through the haze drew back memories of his parent's death and what that water looked like. Drawing his attention back to her, Anika grabbed his wrists and placed his hands on her breasts.

"Fuck me," Anika told Slade, grinding her hips. "Fuck me like I'm not your sister."

He groaned, squeezing her breasts remorselessly. She didn't cry out in pain, but moaned before pressing her lips against his. Her tongue slithered its way into his mouth, feeling like an eel. He moaned, becoming a little panicked about the water's depth, but couldn't resist her.

She pressed her lips hard against his while moving her hands to his chest, pushing him down. Her pussy squeezed his dick so violently that it was bordering on agonizing. Forgetting about the water until he felt it climbing up his back, he allowed her slowly to lower him into it.

Slade released her breasts to grab the sides of the tub. Nope! Too much! Panic became overwhelming him as the water seemed to take on a cloudy green hue. His terror was beyond anything he'd ever felt, making his stomach rile with nausea and pain. While practically out of his own mind with fear, he bit down on Anika's lip. He tasted a flow of blood, but she didn't pull her face away from him. Her mouth ground hard against his, pushing his head down until he felt the water rising to his ears, then cheeks.

TOO MUCH FUCKING WATER. It was too late, though. He found himself under the water, struggling to sit up against her immeasurable strength. Her hands felt like ice, grabbing him and pulling him down to her. Somehow, they had flipped over, with her beneath him, clutching him through the muck and murkiness of the drab water.

Her pussy squeezing the life from his cock. Bubbles slipped from his mouth as he screamed in pain against her mouth. When he broke free from her mouth, he realized Anika looked older, far older than she actually was. Older than him. It wasn't Anika attacking him, but his mother forcing him under the water, trying to keep him with her. He flailed and fought harder than he thought possible. His hands clawed and punched at his mother, desperate to return to his little sister. If he gave in and allowed this psychotic bitch to have her way, he'd fail to protect Anika!

His feet banged into the sides and base of the tub as he fought. The banging was so loud it rippled the world around until he sat up, gagging and choking. The pain around his cock was excruciating.

Slade's crimson eyes snapped open. He found himself on his abdomen, face planted on his bedroom floor and his hand around his dick in a death grip as if trying to strangle the life from the damn thing. He struggled with the urge to scream out in horror.

His hand unclenched, allowing the blood flow to retreat so it could go limp, though it seemed content to remain semi-erect against his will. Another knock at the door made him flinch.

"What?!" he snapped, not intending to.

"Good morning, Slade. I love you." His sister whimpered on the other side of his door.

"Yeah." He growled, trembling. "Go away."

"Okay. I um. Don't forget that I have a swim meet after school today."

"Sure," he grumbled, listening for her to leave as he tried to process the fact that he somehow passed out on his floor and slept the entire night in moments.

It would be another long day. He had to go out in public to ensure she didn't die during her swim meeting. It always felt like the water was preparing to claim them and return them to their drowned parents.

"I love you too," he whispered into the darkness of his depressing bedroom, knowing she'd already left the house.

He laid his head back down on the floor, closed his eyes and breathed deep, relieved to know that his sister was innocent, his mother was dead, and that the entire experience was just a nightmare.

7

THE STORY OF WATER
Anika Darling

The day had been rather uneventful for her. She attended all her classes, even though the school year was nearly over, and she'd been accepted to a local university. She didn't even have to move out of her and Slade's family home and she could stay home more often with the new schedule she'd have for secondary education. Waiting to graduate was nearly agonizing.

Another boy asked her to prom. She politely declined, saying she wasn't allowed to have relations with boys until she was thirty. The faces boys made when she said things like that so sweetly were kind of enjoyable. People would always talk about how mature she was, and that she had an old soul. Eventually, newcomers would find out about her parents because of how a small town worked at the rumor mill. Everyone would immediately act as if that were some sort of explanation for everything she did.

The end of the school day took far too long to arrive, but when it did, she practically ran next door to the swimming pool. The town was small, and after the high school burned down, a local inn with an indoor swimming pool was purchased to replace it. Oddly enough, it worked out well for her slight obsession with water.

Anika took her time in the change room. The thought that a certain someone might have gotten a camera in there made her feel warm and excited in ways she couldn't describe. She stood there, naked, facing the direction she assumed the camera would be.

"Nadine, what are you waiting for? Sex is so much fun," she heard one of her teammates encouraging another.

Anika turned toward the pair, placing her hand on her hips as she cocked her head to the side. Torren lost her virginity at fifteen and since then, she slept with half of each sports team. The girl certainly had a type to go along with her unfathomable appetite.

"I- uh. I'm waiting." Nadine said the same line Anika often used.

"For?" Torren tilted her head forward, staring at her through long blond eyelashes.

"I dunno. I guess... for someone who wants me so bad they don't take 'no' for an answer."

Anika's jaw dropped, and Torren slowly shook her head with wide eyes. The innocent expression on Nadine's face said it all. The girl did not know what she was actually hoping for.

"You know, there's a word for that," Torren told Nadine before a mischievous smirk pulled at the corners of her mouth. "You could always find someone like that in dark alleyways, seedy bars, or dimly lit streets in the dangerous areas of big cities."

The snort came out of Anika whether or not she wanted it to. "Statistically, she's more likely to face sexual assault or raped by a family member."

"What?" Nadine responded with a gasp, likely realizing what her statement was insinuating.

"Huh," Torren yelped, turning to face Anika, who hadn't realized that those statistics weren't common knowledge.

They'd feel utterly horrified to find her search history. The search engine could find anything and she had a lot of questions about everything. Her interests seemed extremely varied.

"Really?" Torren questioned with raised eyebrows, but continued after Anika nodded. "That's a creepy thought."

Anika looked over at Nadine and cocked an eyebrow before speaking to the naïve virgin. "Who would have guessed someone so innocent would be into something so dark?"

"You kinky bitch." Torren added to the teasing.

"That's not exactly what I meant. I-I wanna lose it." Nadine argued. "But I'm scared and I figured it could be like ripping off a Band-Aid."

"Well, let me tell you. Don't do it with a loser from this school."

Nadine blurted out curiously. "Because you did them all?"

Anika snorted softly. What made it funnier was because sweet Nadine didn't seem to realize what she was insinuating. The poor girl meant the comment innocently.

While the others chatted, Anika slipped on her swimsuit. It was so tight around her thighs that she had to wiggle her legs while pulling hard on the elastic material.

"You want an older man, cause they know how to touch you. The first time I orgasmed was with a man ten years older than me."

"The only older guy I know is Anika's brother. I guess he's hot, but he's also creepy." Nadine's eyes flashed to Anika before giving her an apologetic look. "He says nothing to anyone and sits there at every practice with pictures of their parents, even though Anika says she hated them."

"Everyone knows it's just so that no one sits next to him."

"Really? Why doesn't he give up the charade?"

Torren giggled before responding, "Because someone might sit next to him."

Listening to the two chit-chat about Slade made her wonder if there was audio on the device he had taken her pictures with.

After a moment of silence, Nadine finally broke and whimpered, "How could an older guy possibly want someone like me? I don't even have tits."

"You have a pussy, and that's all they are after. It's easier than you think to seduce a guy." Torren advised.

"Wouldn't that be weird if your friend slept with your brother?" Nadine suddenly asked Anika with furrowed eyebrows.

"Why would it be? Actually, the thought of my friend losing her virginity to him is hot. Too bad neither of you have brothers."

Both girls giggled and Torren piped up. "My dad is single."

"Your dad cannot compare to my brother." Anika quickly responded, trying to shake the picture of Torren's four-hundred-pound old man from her mind.

"True that." She laughed and winked at Anika.

The coach's voice suddenly sounded, echoing in the change room, making all three yelp and cover their exposed parts.

"Common ladies, time for practice!" his voice rebound off the stone walls. "This isn't a social hour. Get out here, or I'll send a mom in to collect you."

"Later!" Anika adjusted her shoulder straps before grabbing her swim cap and running out of the change room, leaving her locker wide open.

Why would they try to plan the other girl losing her virginity in such a way? No. It didn't matter, it wasn't her business. As her feet slapped the cement in the swimming area, her eyes scanned the faces of the many parents sitting in the stands. With it getting closer to the last competition, more adults came to encourage their offspring. Her brother was the only guardian who could attend every single practice, though only Friday's were open to the public. When she joined the swim team, it amazed the coach how good she was and really wanted her on the team. In order to protect her, Slade showed up every time she had a swim meet. The coach went to the principal, and the siblings received a summons to discuss this issue.

As he argued the point stating for the fourth time that she wasn't allowed to swim if he wasn't in attendance, Anika lost her self-control. Tears rolled freely down her cheeks. She wanted to swim! But instead of insisting that, she whimpered about how their parents drowned in front of them and it was the only time she felt close to their mum and dad again. Slade's face darkened. It was clear he didn't like sharing that little detail. She made him more pissed off by insisting that he saved her life and probably feared that if he wasn't there, she'd drown, too. The principal told her to go back to class and insisted the adults talk without her, as this was clearly too emotional for her. It didn't matter; she planted the seed and would get her way.

There he was! She raised her hand over her head and waved with a huge smile on her lips. He was sour and glum as usual, with dark bags under his eyes as if he hadn't slept in days. He nodded slowly to her in greeting. There was plenty of space on each side of him, even though the benches were full of parents. It was probably pictures of their parents in those spots. The other adults knew not to disturb the framed memorabilia. Her swim meets were the only times he brought those pictures out of wherever he kept them hidden.

"Hey, Ani," Torren's voice rang out from behind her.

She looked over her shoulder and slowed her pace.

"Ani?" she repeated, feeling slightly disturbed by the sudden use of a nickname after years of 'friendship' with Torren.

"Nadine wants to become closer with some of her friends, so I thought she could have a sleepover at your house tonight."

"Why not your house?"

"After today's meeting, my family and I are going out of state for the summer. Coach already knows I won't be at the tournament."

"That's too bad. Using psychological warfare, our team stood a better chance of winning. Especially with everyone knowing you fucked half our opponents' boyfriends."

Torren threw her head back and laughed. Her D-cups bounded slightly in response. How could that girl always look so sexually appealing? Half the parents in the stands avoided even glancing in her direction because everyone watching knew what they were looking at. She pinched her elbows together, engorging her breasts between them as she pulled Anika's arm into an embrace. Even her tight swimsuit wasn't enough to contain those things.

"Please let her go to your place."

Her eyes darted down to where her arm disappeared between Torren's tits. How could she really say no to that? Her gaze met Torren's before she gave one more half hearted attempt at denial.

"Her parents would never approve. I'm amazed your parents did one time, considering the way all the adults see Slade as too young to be considered an adult."

"She's going to tell them she's at my house, and just walk over to your place instead." Torren put her arm around Nadine's shoulders, while the other girl blushed. "We got it all planned out. All you gotta do is say yes."

Anika gave a snort. "You're a bad influence, you know?"

Giggling, Torren moved so her arms could wrap around Anika, still with her breasts trapping that one arm. To an onlooker, it appeared to be two young girls simply being affectionate. For Anika, it almost felt like Torren was trying to seduce her or use sex-appeal to get what she wanted.

"And what if Slade says no?"

Anika smirked at the other girl as she threw down her last line of defense. He would say 'no' if she told him to.

"Hunny, I've known you since we were little. Your brother has never said 'no' to you."

While Torren and Anika talked, Nadine had vanished to speak with her parents. She approached unnoticed by both of them.

With wide eyes, Nadine interjected. "Never? Even though he's raising you?"

"I don't often put him in a position where he needs to say it." Anika responded defensively with narrowed eyes.

"You guys have a bit of a weird dynamic, don't you?" Nadine questioned, tilting her head to the side.

"Fine, you can sleep over, but that's the last time you talk about how weird the dynamic between us is. Understand?"

"I do, I'm sorry. I have no right to talk about it, cause I could never understand what you've been through."

"You could." She said in a flat voice, taking a step away before talking over her shoulder. "*Your* parents could still die."

As she marched toward the other swimmers, she could hear Nadine behind her. "She hates me now. I'm so stupid. I shouldn't have said anything about it."

"Don't worry, she's not really hurt." Torren comforted Nadine, nearly out of earshot. "Anika's a bit of a narcissist."

Anika stopped walking and listened carefully to the conversation, though kept her back on the pair, hoping they didn't notice she could still hear them.

She turned her face to the benches and called out, "Hey, Slade! I'm going to kick butt today!"

He gave her a nod, though his cheeks reddened as if he wished she hadn't drawn the entire stadium's attention to him. Sometimes, he was just too damn cute. Even though she called out to her brother, her attention was solely on Torren's response to Nadine.

"Really? How can you be such close friends with her, then?"

"It's a mental disorder. She's not like that on purpose, but it also means that I'm very careful about what I say and do around her because anything can control or manipulate me."

"Control you?" Nadine questioned, sounding genuinely afraid, which was what made Anika more annoyed than it should have.

She sighed and turned on her heels. When the pair saw her eyes on them, Nadine's mouth hung open and her eyes widened. Torren crossed her arms beneath her breasts and smirked at her. The big-breasted bitch totally did that on purpose. She marched back to the others.

"Don't worry, I'm in therapy and have prescriptions. I won't do anything that will cause you hardship and I enjoy having friends and people around me." Anika tilted her head to the side, knowing her demeanor had changed from that bubbly, energetic girl to someone serious and slightly intimidating. "It's useful for me to surround myself with socialites because it looks good for university. I won't do anything to risk how the world views me, but yes. If you want to be close to me, it's something you'll have to come to accept. I'm not the same as I pretend to be... But neither is anyone else. Everyone wears masks and hides who they are from the public... I'm just better at it."

She turned on her heels and marched to where the coach was instructing the others. While the middle-aged man blathered about competition and team spirit, Anika noticed Nadine glancing at her several times through the corner of her eye. If that girl became too nervous, it could be detrimental to the façade that Anika had built up around herself. Why did Torren have to open her whore mouth?! She kept a warm smile painted on her lips, though her thoughts were a dark contrast. Her brother was weird because he lacked social skills. However, she masked so perfectly that it was rare for anyone to notice that he was relatively normal in comparison.

Her eyes shifted to her brother, and she purposefully made her smile bigger. Things were about to get complicated. She could feel it in her gut. Something was wrong. He appeared bored as always, but the bags under his eyes screamed of mental and physical exhaustion. Had he slept all day? He looked awful.

The coach called her name for the second time, pulling her from her deep train of thought. She turned to face him with raised eyebrows before giving him a toothy grin.

"Of course, coach!" Her enthusiastic acknowledgement wasn't out of character for the person who everyone thought she was.

Anika practically skipped across the large space to the starting line. This was the last practice before the competition. She smirked over at her brother, who no longer looked bored. He sat on the edge of his wooden seat with narrowed eyes as he watched her prepare to dive into the deep water. Something about the way he stared made her so much more excited about finally swimming. She even felt her nipples grow hard beneath the tight spandex of her suit.

Bang! The gunshot announced the commencement of the race and Anika hit the water. Nothing else in the world existed the moment she broke the surface. The shimmering liquid swirled around her, touching every inch of flesh, visible or not. Studying to be an underwater welder not only meant a fantastic income, but she'd be in the water nearly every day. Slade was going to have a heart attack when he found out.

She kept her legs together and ground her hips to make her body wave, which pushed her to the surface. Taking that first gasp of air was like being born alive once again. It was a breath she stole that the water would never take from her. She would defeat the water every day for the rest of her life if she could.

Anika kicked her legs and shifted her arms movements as if dancing with the water's surface. She planned and practiced every movement with timed perfection. She swam down the line and back.

Her hand grabbed the ribbed edge of the pool and pulled her head from the water. Her blue eyes darted to the large overhead sign with their names and waited patiently for their times to appear. It took her only moments to realize she came in at a close second behind Nadine.

"Good job!" she exclaimed to the girl who had beaten her by mere seconds.

Holding the side of the pool, Anika released her bladder, while making eye contact with the new student, who was busy thanking her. The buildup of an entire day's worth of urine invisibly warmed the water around her legs. She'd been pissing in the pool pretty much every second day since she made the team. It turned out that the water changing color because of urine was a myth. Since she tested it, she realized that pissing in the pool gave her some strange rush that she just couldn't explain.

Once she was done and certain there'd be no yellow streaking down her inner thighs from the remaining piss caught in her swimsuit, she climbed out of the pool. She walked over to Nadine and offered her a hand to climb out. Nadine raised her eyebrows before taking Anika's hand.

With an expression of surprise, the girl took Anika's hand. "You're way nicer than I thought a narcissist could be."

Anika pulled herself from the pool and stepped in close to Nadine while wrapping her arms around the other girl. "Don't say that too loud," she was smiling, but her voice was sharp.

"Sorry." Nadine wrapped her arms lightly around Anika, almost timidly.

"Come on, don't look so upset." Anika pulled away, but kept her arm across Nadine's shoulders to guide her toward the others who were waiting their turn. "Be happy, you kicked ass that round."

Nadine beamed with pride. "You really think so?"

"Of course! You even beat me."

They were definitely going to have fun later... if Nadine had the guts to lie to her parents and show up to sleep at her house that night.

8

Anxiety Pangs
Slade Darling

There was something absolutely horrifying about deep water and the way it swallowed up any who entered. When one considered how resilient his sister was over their trauma, he wondered if she even remembered it. He felt relieved watching her prance around with her friends after a smooth second place win. She was lucky to be so popular. The other students bullied him in high school, so he didn't attend social groupings or activities because he knew he wasn't wanted.

When the swim meet was finally over, parents left the stands to fetch their offspring. He sat there waiting for her to come to him. He simply felt uncomfortable attempting to mill through the crowd of people as they swarmed to the exits. Besides, Anika was busy with her friends.

"Hey you!" his sweet sister exclaimed, climbing up the benches to reach him in the stands.

"Be careful."

His warning went on deaf ears as she jumped from one seat to the next. He grit his teeth in irritation before cocking his head to the side.

"Go get dressed. I'm going to drop you off at home and then I have an errand to run."

"Hug first!"

That little swimsuit did nothing to hide how drenched her little body was. Instead, water trickled from the thin material and rolled down her skin, making goosebumps rise. Her puffy nipples pushed hard against the spandex, as if in search of warmth to ward off the chill. It was horrible. He rose to his feet, giving an exasperated sigh. She wrapped her arms around him in a tight hug, pressing her icy body against his. He could feel every curve through his sweater. Slade patted the top of her head, struggling against the headache which made this echoing room nearly unbearable. His fingers massaged the temple and behind his earlobe on the right side of his face. The noise wasn't the reason behind his pain, but it didn't help. Slade got a headache every time he came this close to deep water. He always felt sick around large amounts of water, feeling almost as if he and his sister would someday return to that lake's icy embrace.

"I'm so happy you could come watch me again."

"I'm glad, too," his voice was monotone and devoid of emotions as he tried to hide his insecurity. "Please, go get ready."

Anika finally stepped away, before she ran off toward the change room, appearing completely unbothered by the water trickling down her body. With the backs of his fingers, he lightly wiped at the wet swimsuit shaped imprint on his shirt. She would change in a hurry to please him, and then they could finally leave. In the meantime, Slade slowly made his way toward the change room.

"Hi, Mr. Darling." Anika's heavily breasted friend announced, giving him a small smile as her fingers toyed with a strand of wet blonde hair.

Getting called that made him feel slightly gross. He didn't understand why she decided his first name would no longer suffice, considering he had fucked her nearly a year before. After that, she started distancing herself by creating a barrier of titles.

Mr. Darling. Disgusting. Darling had been Anika's father's last name. After his mom married the psycho, they made Slade change his own last name.

He stopped a good 5 paces away from the change room and crossed his arms. Anika wouldn't take too long.

"Have fun tonight," the girl winked playfully before scurrying into the change room.

"Wha-?" he asked, but she bolted into the change room before he could finish that train of thought.

There was definitely something wrong with these teenagers. He stood there pondering what the girl's comment could mean when his sister finally returned.

Anika marched out wearing her towel on her head, carrying both her bookbag and her sports pack. She wore her school uniform, though half the buttons on the shirt weren't done up. The gust of wind from her movements made the material flutter, exposing her navel.

"My swimsuit is getting stinky. Can you wash- what's wrong?" She suddenly stopped walking toward him and cocked her head to the side.

"Your friend said something about tonight..."

"Oh, sorry about that. I forgot to ask you sooner," she tilted her head to the side. "Apparently, Torren suggested Nadine should sleep over. I wasn't really listening."

"Torren? Miss tits?"

"Yeah." His sister giggled at the nickname as she followed him toward the door.

"Why?"

Slade pulled the heavy metal door open and allowed his sister to walk through first. She looked over her shoulder at him with a devilish grin.

"Nadine thinks you're cute."

He gave her a flat stare while following her out the door. Maybe the girl thought he was attractive, but it was just as likely his mischievous little sister was toying with him. They headed to his beat-up little car.

He drove Anika home in relative silence. Once they arrived, he waited in his car at the end of the driveway to ensure she entered the house safely. Slade breathed a sigh of relief as her scent faded from the confined space. Her perfume combined with the smell of the pool made his head spin. He threw his car into gear and drove off. Nearly twenty minutes of driving passed as he made his way to the graveyard near the center of the town.

Slade made a point of trying to visit his parents a few times a month. It wasn't really about mourning their death. More than anything, he needed an excuse to leave the house aside from groceries or errands for his sister. He parked the car and walked across the ancient cemetery covered in grave markers until he found theirs. Their grave was so old that the grass had overgrown the burial site. It simply looked like a part of a field with a tombstone marking the place they rested. 'Dearest Departed' scrawled across the top of the tomb was the first thing he noticed every visit. He had to research what to put on the tombstone so it would seem like he and Anika truly cared that their parents were dead. She didn't even fake crying at their funeral. It was hard to miss people who were never there, and when they were, they abused you.

"Hi," he whispered before sitting down on the grass with his back pressed against the cold tombstone.

The chill that radiated through the back of his t-shirt really made him feel like he was getting a hug from death. With his eyes closed, he could focus on the world around him and attempt to find inner calm. The scent of soil and fresh flowers from the grave next to him was nearly overwhelming. The wind gusted lightly, making his dark hair flutter across his face.

'The blank patches in my memory are getting worse. I'm getting scared. Mom, sometimes I even wish you were here. Or that I let you...' he closed his eyes tightly, remembering the feel of her grabbing him and attempting to keep him under the water with her. *'I've become a monster, just like Anika's dad... and just like mine was before he disappeared.'*

His mom was also a psychopath, though she had seemed relatively harmless. She manipulated his biological father to kill himself. Then she convinced her second husband to join her in death and bring their children with them.

Anika's father had blank spots in his memory too, and committed horrible crimes, forcing Slade to help him. The worst part was, after some time, Slade came to enjoy helping hurt dad's toys. If Slade mentioned the toys when they weren't going down to play with them, the bastard would claim none of it happened and said he didn't understand what the teen was talking about. Eventually, Slade would sneak down and torture the toys without the old man's command.

"We were a disaster waiting to happen," he whispered, with a sarcastic smirk pulling at the corner of his lips.

Since childhood, he has had psychotic tendencies. He remembered taking a family beach trip. It was when he realized his ventures with dad had more of an effect on him than he thought. He held his sister under the water, expecting her to react like dad's victims, but that wasn't what happened. The way she laid there and took it when he expected some sort of fight from her. He could have done anything to her little body, but she accepted his decision as though it were the law. He was a teenager and could have forced that little girl to do anything he wanted. Witnessing her blind acceptance was the first thing that made him feel pure arousal without the need to cause pain. He wondered if she was still so obedient to him she'd obey if he told her to let him fuck her. *No.* He needed to protect her. Even from himself.

He failed to protect her a mere two years later when their parents died. When he woke in the sinking car, she was already terrified and had a large bruise on her forehead. With the quickly rising water, he tried to soothe her, but she cried anyway. The moment she cried, he felt himself come undone. He didn't want her crying; he wanted that same peaceful expression she had when he tried to drown her. Their parents ignored their pleas for help. Once the car was full of water, he simply opened the door. Slade put his sister on his back before he made his way to the surface.

"I'll do whatever I need to," he mumbled, closing his eyes and shaking his head.

"Mr. Darling?" His heart thundered in his ears, wondering if he said all that out loud as his crimson eyes darted in search of the speaker.

"New girl."

"Hi, yeah, I-uh- I'm Nadine."

She was exceptionally pretty, with sea-green eyes and sandy blond hair. Without a swim cap on, her hair hung loose in waves, nearly down to her waist. The light wind made her hair flutter delicately. Her arms wrapped around her torso and she raised her shoulders high, almost making her appear as if she were cringing. She had a small bookbag strap hanging over one shoulder. The girl wore a pretty white dress. The backdrop was a growing darkness as the sun set in the distance. He had laid there far longer than he thought. It was possible that he fell asleep.

"Isn't it a bit too dark for a little girl to be wandering around?"

"Oh, I'm walking to your house. Didn't the girls ask you? Torren said she'd ask-," her face turned crimson as she stopped talking.

The breeze gusted her dress, making it flutter around her legs, which pressed tightly together. Her hands moved to grasp each other in front of her lap. The girl's lips parted as though there was something more she wanted to say.

Torren was the one he fucked the previous year, right before he started having some serious self-control issues. She was an extremely sexual young woman who practically begged him to fuck her. He licked his lips, reminiscing in the memory of the high energy and enthusiastic young woman.

"Tell me what she said." His voice was flat and commanding, though he tried to make sure he seemed warm and welcoming.

"She-" The girl's breaths were heavy pants. "She said she would love to do *it* with you again, if she could, but her parents won't let her sleep out anymore because she got caught having group sex by the police at a party."

The girl with the big tits was legal now, so did it really matter? So was his own sister, but she wasn't allowed to sleep out, go to parties or really do anything without supervision. Though she never even bothered to try.

"That naughty girl wasn't supposed to tell anyone. Please tell me, did she have a good reason for sharing this with you?"

A chilly breeze made her hands move to hold her skirt down. Her little white dress did nothing to hide her nipples hardening beneath the thin material. No bra. Interesting. She slipped the book bag off her shoulder and let it fall to the ground.

"I told her I want to lose my virginity."

While blurting out those words, the girl practically trembled with anxiety. One of her hands self-consciously moved to hide her breasts. Her forearm pressed her dress against those adorable nipples, which he was sure had to be sensitive as hell.

"Are you sure that's what you want?" he questioned, rubbing his arms to clear up the goosebumps that rose from the breeze.

Her eyes lit up with the thrill of what she imagined may happen to her. The young woman looked nervous and excited, but he had very little trust for virgins. All he needed was for the girl to complain that he fucked her or claim it was without permission. He could lose everything. The town folk were annoying and had a hive mind. There was talk after his parents died about how young girls mysteriously stopped going missing. He was smart enough to drive into the nearby city to get his dolls. The way she looked at him reminded him of when Torren asked him to fuck her. That girl was an adventure of flexibility.

"If you want me to take your virginity, remove your underwear."

If he thought she was blushing before, it was far worse after his demand. Her features were on fire. Her head turned just a fraction, as if considering saying no. If she did, this entire thing would end immediately. Even though he was already horny and wanted to violate every part of her tiny body, taking a girl from the area was too much of a risk.

"Here? Now?"

He cocked an eyebrow and nodded to confirm her fears. It was dark enough that unless someone flashed a light into the graveyard, no one would see them.

Slade basked in her discomfort, watching as her trembling hands slid up her outer thighs to her hips, dragging her skirt with them. He remained seated, leaning back against the tombstone, enjoying the glimpse of her pale thighs. Her hands finally reached her hips, so those dainty little fingers could curl over the waistband of her white underwear. She slowly peeled it down. Her movements were jarring and hesitant. When she bent over to remove them from her legs, he could see right down the neckline of her dress to those perky little titties.

The girl stood straight with a red face and balled the underwear tightly in her hand. She stared over at him with wide eyes and her bottom lip pulled into her mouth.

"You're very tiny," he purred, enjoying the thought of bending her over and fucking the virginity from every hold she had.

"My mom says I'm built for swimming and jockeying."

"That, you are."

She put her balled fist behind her back, as if having it out to site would make it less embarrassing for her. Her legs pulled tight together so her little flat, slipper-style shoes pulled close together, nearly atop each other.

"Smell them."

"What?"

"If you can't handle even the slightest of humiliations, I don't think you're going to enjoy sex, and that makes the thought of fucking you uncomfortable."

With flames in her cheeks, the girl brought her fist to her face and took a slow, deep breath. Her eyes lit up as if she smiled behind her hand.

She sounded surprised. "Smells like laundry detergent."

He smirked, slightly annoyed and a little disappointed by how easily she appeared to relax. "Throw them away. They are going to stay here as a reminder of what you're about to do."

She took a step and threw them. But they didn't travel far. They unbundled and landed atop of tombstone, hanging so the little pink bow he hadn't noticed before was completely visible. She gasped and took two steps.

"Don't move."

She froze, looking over her shoulder at Slade, who continued to smirk. Her lips parted as if she wanted to say something, but couldn't bring herself to do anything more.

"Pull up your dress and show me your pussy."

Her eyes widened, and she stared around.

"We are in a graveyard!"

"I hadn't noticed."

"I thought we were going to go to your house."

"So, we can do it in front of my sister? Aren't you a little freak?"

"No, that's not what I meant. We are-."

"Don't worry about it," he raised his hand to underline his mother's name on the tombstone behind him. "My parents would enjoy the show."

Her mouth hung open as she processed what he said. Everyone knew he was an orphan, but the silly young woman probably didn't even realize why he was there.

"I-I can't."

"Then clearly, you don't really want it."

"Wait-..." she grabbed the hem of her skirt and dragged it up, gradually exposing her thighs until gloriously her naked pussy.

"You have no hair?"

"I shaved it for you. I thought. If you agreed, I didn't know what you liked and worried that if there was any hair there, you wouldn't like it."

"I don't care if the property has foliage as long as it's maintained." He frowned thoughtfully before adding. "For the future, remember that it's your body and how you maintain it needs to feel comfortable for you. If a partner doesn't like it, that's up to them to contend with."

Her cheeks were on fire. "I didn't enjoy shaving, and it's really itchy."

"Get an electric clipper if you want it to appear cleaned up without the razor burn."

She nodded slowly. Her hands still trembled, already tired from holding the hem of her skirt up so he could see her pussy. However, after conversing, the girl seemed to have come to terms with her humiliation and relaxed a little. Her breathing slowed, and though her cheeks were red, she no longer looked like she was going to faint.

"Tell me what you've done with a guy."

"Kiss. On the lips."

"Don't lower your skirt. Come closer, I can barely see you from there." As she sauntered toward him, closing the four-grave gap, he resumed his discussion. "Have you ever watched porn?"

Now her face was on fire. "Yes."

"What did you search for?"

"I- urm," she paused in both her speech and her walk.

"Telling me will help make you more aroused."

He didn't know if it would get her more horny, but her torment certainly was making his cock press against his jogging pants to an uncomfortable degree. Soon, he'd need to adjust, so it didn't dangle down his pant leg, but he didn't want to draw her attention to it yet.

"doing-it-in-a-pool."

The snort wasn't on purpose, and he instantly regretted it when she lowered her dress a little. The girl's eyebrows drew together and her shoulders slumped. She pouted and let the hem of her skirt slip from her fingers so it could waver in the light breeze.

"Don't do that. Now you need to be punished. I told you to hold it up, didn't I?"

"Yes?.. but..." her hands snatched up the fluttering hem of her skirt and raised it.

"Now hold it higher. Show me those little tits."

The girl whimpered before her eyebrows drew down. Her elbows drew inward as if trying to squeeze the small amount of fat on her chest to increase its mass. Young women had so many body insecurities and for no reason. He would enjoy her tits if they were completely nonexistent, just as he would if they were massive.

"I won't spend my entire evening comforting you." He put his hand through his dark, silky hair. "Either you want to do this, or you don't."

"They're so small, I just don't understand why you want to see them."

"This little show is more about you than it is about me."

"When you took off your underwear, how did it make you feel?"

"Embarrassed..." Her hands trembled, struggling to hold her skirt so he could still see her pussy.

"And now look at you, acting like the deviant little girl you are, holding your dress up for every ghost in this place to see."

The gullible girl's eyes widened before her head swiveled back and forth in search of the disembodied souls Slade spoke of. He chuckled in the back of his throat while signaling for her to approach.

"So, pull it higher. Show me how bad you want to give up your virginity." As he spoke, he crossed his legs at the ankle to try hiding his massively hard cock.

She nodded and pulled her dress to her chin, exposing every inch of that pearl-colored flesh. Her nipples were as hard as he suspected, looking like succulent little nubs of untouched pleasures.

"Do you touch yourself?"

"What?" She twitched, nearly dropping the material in her hands.

"When you're watching porn, do you masturbate?"

"Sometimes..." her voice came out a timid mumble.

Mere steps away from him, she stopped. He could see enough details in the dim light that he didn't bother to encourage her to approach further.

"Show me."

Her tense grip on the dress turned her knuckles white. "What?"

"I want to see how you touch yourself. How am I to know what you like if you don't show me?" He feigned innocence and cocked his head to the side. "I want to pleasure you properly, so I need you to do this."

The girl would feel utterly devastated if she started touching herself and he simply walked away. His eyes shimmered with malice. She brought her hands down, which also hid her body from view before her fingers pressed into the space between her thighs.

"I can't see anything."

Two more small steps brought her to his side. Her dress still blocked his view.

"I still can't see." She tried to lift her dress with one hand while pushing her fingers between the lips of her delicious looking pussy.

"You could tuck your dress under your chin." He told her and reached out with one hand so his fingers could wrap around her ankle. "There you go, just like that. Now use one hand to pull your lips open. I want to see all of you." He smirked as the girl obeyed so easily. "Good girl." He purred before adding, "You look beautiful."

Her breathing turned into uneven gasps for air. She drew her bottom lip into her mouth, somehow reminding him so much of his sister that his boner became a raging pain. He was trying to escape his thoughts of Anika for a little while, and even while getting laid, she was on his mind.

His hand slid up the back of her leg, enjoying the delicate curvature of her swimmer's muscles. "Now, use one finger from your other hand to touch yourself. That's it. Look at you, good girl."

She whimpered lightly when her own dainty fingers touched her tiny clit. Having her chin tilted down to hold her dress meant that if she opened her eyes, she'd have to watch her fingers work their magic. His hand made his way up to the back of her knee, where his fingers lightly tickled the sensitive skin before trailing back down her calf. It was a struggle not to lick his lips or simply bury his face into that delicious-looking pussy. Alas, the girl didn't look as if she knew exactly what she wanted, and he didn't need any problems with her parents.

"Tell me what you want from this encounter."

"To lose my virginity." She kept her eyes tightly shut.

"How do you want to do that?"

She opened her eyes, with her brows pulled down before responding, "Urm. Sex?"

"Sex isn't all about ramming a cock inside you."

"It isn't?" Her breathing became gradually heavier, increasing the faster her hand moved.

"It's about enjoying your body and that of another." His explanation was meant as a lesson, but it was probably lost on the silly girl.

"But unless your thing goes in mine, I'll still be a virgin."

She suddenly gasped and placed both hands against her pussy, allowing her dress to flutter down around her. Her eyes were as wide as they could go. Maybe this was her first orgasm. She looked too surprised to have much experience.

"What's wrong?"

"I have to go to the washroom."

She moved as if she was about to step away, but his hand on her ankle clenched. He didn't let her slip free. The girl dropped her gaze to his grasp on her. Her mouth hung open in a moment of panic. Those dainty hands balled into fists, clenching at the hem of her pretty little dress. The more tense she became, the whiter her knuckles turned.

"That's not pee." Slade sighed softly, shaking his head as his hand slowly trailed toward her thigh. "Let me show you pleasure."

"But it feels like I have to pee."

He let go of her leg and rose to his feet. His hands delicately cupped her face as he stared down into those pretty doe eyes. His thumb delicately traced her bottom lip, considering kissing her, but deciding to hold off.

"It's not pee." When she looked confused, he continued, "It's called cumming. Men and women both can cum from pleasure." When she looked skeptical, he frowned and added thoughtfully, "If you want me to take your virginity, you must trust me on this."

"Okay." Her voice was a muted whisper as she lifted her dress to tuck it beneath her chin. "Do you want me to touch myself more?"

"*I* want to touch you. Would you like that?"

She nodded slowly, dropping the hem of her dress from beneath her chin. Her cheeks regained their blush to a fierce degree. She drew her bottom lip into her mouth and inched closer, so her small breasts could press against him.

He smirked down at her, "Pardon? I didn't hear you."

"Please. Please touch me." Her hand moved forth and grabbed the hem of his t-shirt as if trying to pull him closer to her.

"Okay." He slipped his hands around her waist, grinding his body against hers.

She gasped, bowing her head so even if he wanted to kiss her, he couldn't. His hands wandered up and down her body, enjoying the small curves. He ventured up her waist, down her arms, and up her backside. Her skin was silk beneath his gentle touch. His hands were smooth and uncalloused from a lack of hard labor.

"Hold that pretty dress of yours up for the world to see," he encouraged.

Feeling the soft cotton material beneath his fingers shift, he slipped his hands from her waist to grab her bare ass.

He buried his face into her neck and breathed deep, enjoying the combined scent of her floral perfume and swimming pool chlorine. Slade moaned lightly before pressing his lips to the sensitive skin there. When she felt his boner through his jogging pants, she whimpered, flinching away from it. For a girl who wanted to lose her virginity, she certainly feared a dick.

His selfishness was the only reason he didn't ask more questions at that moment. He gripped her ass tightly and pulled her hard against him, so his cock ground against her stomach. Lifting her, he turned and set her down on his parent's tombstone.

"It's going to be okay," he purred in comfort to her, breaking up his words with light kisses as he moved his face down her body.

When he got to that tiny, untouched nipple, he licked it, dragging the flat of his tongue right across it. He paid special attention to her reaction. She gasped but didn't pull away, so his next step was to pull it tenderly into his mouth and pinch it between his lips, rolling it around as he moved his jaw back and forth. She gasped and whimpered loudly, twitching beneath his touch. Slade smirked before moving his lips in a line of kisses to her other nipple. Instead of simply taunting this one, he pulled it full force, suckling hard, while his hand moved to the other saliva-soaked nipple to toy with it, pinching it between his thumb and forefinger.

Her arms shook from strain, but being a swimmer, she had muscles most girls didn't and could handle continuing to hold up her dress. While he suckled and toyed with her body, little goosebumps formed and spread across her skin. Her knees pulled tight, trapping him between her thighs as she let out another whimpering moan.

He smiled against her skin before receding downward, trailing tender kisses across her ribs, then across her navel until he found that delicious virgin pussy he'd been anticipating.

Settling one knee into the graveyard soil, he leaned his chest against the tombstone. His hands rested behind her ass, offering extra support. Without giving her a chance to squirm or say anything they'd regret, he slammed his face between those small lips in search of that little pleasure button. The moment his tongue and lips claimed her clit, she yelped, nearly screaming in surprise.

He barely settled into a rhythm when she gasped and her thighs tried to squeeze his head into oblivion. The material from her dress fluttered down around his head, hiding him from sight. Her warm fingers clutched at her skirt and his hair beneath as she convulsed from his touch.

"Wait. Oh!" Clearly, she was about to orgasm and there was no way he would slow down until she did. "Stop, I have to pee. I can't! This is too embarrassing."

Nothing would stop Slade from making her finish. He felt her stomach muscles tense against his forehead while the muscles in her legs spasmed and strained, making her toes curl. Her clit went stiff beneath his tongue as his well-practiced piece of machinery masterfully labored away.

"No! no! It's coming out!"

It started in a trickle, which only emphasized the amount of control Nadine had over her body. Her hips bucked lightly. He moaned, slurping up and swallowing as much of her liquid as he could, when it finally streamed from her. The salty, sweet flavor was his heavenly reward for a job well done. When it ended, the girl sat there twitching and struggling to breathe.

He stood while sliding his hands up her thighs, taking her dress with them. He wrapped his arms around her, following her smooth skin with his fingers until he could hold her against him. His cock practically ached with the need to erupt as he pressed it through his jogging pants against her pussy.

She flinched away from it with one of her hands moving to press against the center of his chest.

Her hesitation was too much for him, so Slade gave a soft sigh. "I don't believe you're as ready as you think you are."

There were too many variables with this one. The police would investigate her last known location, and she was supposed to sleep at his house. He couldn't just do whatever he wanted with her. Too many risks made this little doll a pain to pursue.

"How about this?" He offered, pressing his pussy moistened lips to her temple. "Later tonight, if you still want to go all the way, you can come see me."

"But, but I'm ready. I promise I am. I don't want to go to college and still be a virgin."

"Sure, you are." He cooed and pressed her hard against himself to lift her and place her on her feet in front of him.

"Please!" she begged, looking a little more desperate.

He distracted her. "You came all over my parent's tombstone."

She gasped, turning to stare at the liquid splattering in heavy trails down the gray engraved rock. Her gaze shifted to the wet area down the front of his shirt.

"I- I." the silly girl stuttered out in a mixture of embarrassment and panic.

He chuckled softly and pressed his lips to hers to silence her.

When Slade broke off the kiss, he purred in her ear, "It was sexy as fuck."

He released his grasp on her and stepped away, grinning down at her red face. He spun on his heels and marched away, toward the parking lot. She followed quickly, like the good little bitch she was.

9

THERE BE THREE
Anika Darling

The others arriving together was the one thing she never considered a possibility. She stood there at the entrance to the kitchen, watching the pair walk in. Her friend's face would heat every time she looked up at Slade, who seemed his usual oblivious self. Maybe they fucked already, but then again, maybe they didn't.

It would take some serious acting for Anika to hide her disappointment. The pair even looked like they would make a cute couple. Nadine kept glancing over her shoulder at Slade, and every time she did, her cheeks would redden. They each faced the two opposite walls of the narrow entryway, leaning against them to remove their shoes.

"Welcome home!" she exclaimed and excitedly bolted down the hall to her brother, who was wiggling his foot into his house slipper.

She went to wrap her arms around him but froze, looking at his chest with a dark gray patch across his shirt.

"Your clothes are wet." Anika gasped, flinching away from

Slade, but kept her hands resting on his hips.

"Does that mean you don't want a hug?"

"Yes," she pouted. "Of course, I do!"

He slipped his arms around her and pulled her into a hug, his hand pressing against the back of her head, so her cheek pushed against the moist area of his shirt. It was cool against her warm face, and he smelled like a strange mix of something earthy and sweet. When he finally let her pull away enough that she could stare up at him curiously, he leaned down and pressed his lips against her forehead before smirking down at her.

"You smell like pee," she blurted out, not meaning to say anything at all.

Her eyebrows rose to make the statement seem more innocent.

Slade laughed while Nadine gasped, bringing her hands up to cover her mouth. It was as she thought. That was okay. It wasn't as if she had any say in what her brother did... or who.

"I'm going to the basement." His voice was flat and emotionless.

Clearly, he wanted time alone, without these young girls bugging him, but she had barely seen him all day. Just a small amount of attention would suffice.

"Please eat dinner first. I made everyone supper. I worked really hard."

Her brows furrowed and shoulders slumped forward. He stared at her, and then toward the basement door. When his dark eyes shifted back to her face again, she pushed her bottom lip out in a slight pout. He rolled his eyes before turning away. He slid his other foot into its slipper.

Anika took Nadine's hand and gave her a big, warm smile.

"You're hungry, aren't you? I made dinner. I was hoping we could eat as a family. It's been a long time..."

Nadine's eyebrows rose in surprise, but she quickly agreed. "Of course, I am. I only had a little dinner with my parents before leaving."

Nadine turned to face Anika with a wavering smile. Anika was disturbed by how clammy the other girl's hand felt in hers. Maybe Nadine was too nervous about her nefarious plans to eat a decent amount under her parents' watchful eyes.

"I'm surprised your parents let you sleep here." Anika announced, looking over her shoulder at the shorter girl. "Cause everyone thinks my brother's too young to be a guardian, even though he raised me for my entire life."

"Oh, they think I'm sleeping at- your entire life?"

"Yeah," they walked past the wide opening to the living room and entered the kitchen area so Anika could lead her to a chair with a waiting bowl of cheesy noodles. "Even before they died, my brother took care of me. I think it was a few years before they passed away that he took on that responsibility."

Slade, who had his hand hovering over the keypad for the basement, froze. He seemed a little annoyed, but turned toward the table, took a few paces to close the distance and plopped down in his seat.

"You're going to eat with us?!" Anika exclaimed, sounding far too excited.

The place settings were perfect, and she even folded the tissue paper napkins to make little pockets for holding the utensils.

"Can we have ice cream for dessert?"

"You may. Then you need to shower and wash the pool's chemicals off you."

"I showered at hom-."

Anika interrupted, not wanting Nadine to upset Slade by arguing, "You should shower anyway. You are covered in dirt."

Maybe the girl hadn't noticed the dirt on her legs, dress, and forearms. Nadine lifted her arm to stare at it in surprise.

"We could shower together to save time before bed, just like in the locker room." Nadine's mouth hung open slightly in surprise, but Anika didn't give her the chance to respond or argue. "It's going to be so much fun! I haven't had a sleepover in almost a year."

"Eat." Slade grumbled, taking his third bite of dinner.

"Yes." Anika responded excitedly and quickly shoved a large bite of noodles into her mouth.

As she ate, she watched the dynamic between the other two. Subtle glances from Nadine followed by blushing. Slade looked over his shoulder at the basement door. It was sad that she was more jealous of a basement than she was of her friend sleeping with her brother.

"It's very good, Anika." Nadine tried to break the awkward silence.

"Oh, you're very welcome. I cook dinner every few days to take the load off my brother. He works so hard every day." She beamed with pride at the man who had a sizeable chunk of porkchop on his fork about to enter his mouth.

Slade cocked an eyebrow at her and she grinned back, knowing that she seemed far too happy about Nadine being there. It was fine. No one would suspect a thing. She couldn't believe how sweet the other girl was. It made her excited about the quality time they would share.

The rest of the dinner passed in a drowning silence, where she planned her interview with Nadine. She needed to know everything about what it was like and if it hurt her or if it was pure pleasure. Taking her last few bites from her plate, she quickly stood and carried her plate over to the sink.

"I'll do the dishes tonight." Anika offered, smirking at her brother. "To thank you for letting me have a sleepover."

Slade grunted softly and shoved the last bite of his dinner into his mouth. He rubbed his eyes with his left hand and gave a long, relieved-sounding sigh before standing.

"Here," he handed her the plate with one hand while the other moved to the small of her back. "Be good."

His hand felt like an icicle radiating a chill through the thin material of her shirt. His breath was hot on her cheek, making goosebumps raise down her neck. She turned her face toward him as she collected his plate. He kissed her on the forehead again. Anika closed her eyes, taking a deep breath to enjoy the familial moment, but all she could smell was sweet urine from his shirt, which was barely masked by the smell of cheesy noodles.

"We will!" she assured him as she flicked on the water and turned her attention to the hot liquid splashing across the dirty dishes.

Watching her brother leave into the basement from the corner of her eye, Anika felt a pang of worry. Sighing, she turned her attention to Nadine, who still sat at the table.

"Are you almost done?"

"Yep."

"Yes?" she corrected, sounding a lot like her brother.

"Uh-huh." Nadine picked up her plate and carried it over to Anika by the sink.

As she took the other girl's dirty dishes, she also picked up the dish towel from where it hung and held it out. "If you don't mind helping?"

"Of course not." Nadine gave her a big smile as she took the dry rag. "Do you mind if I just dry them and set them on the table?"

That irked her a little. What was the point of having Nadine help at all if Anika was just going to follow her to clean up? No. It was not the time to be a snot.

"Of course you can."

As Anika washed the dishes, she began her line of questioning. "So, tell me what happened."

"What happened where?"

Nadine really couldn't be that dense. "With my brother."

"Do you really want to know?"

"Didn't Torren tell you?"

"Yeah, she said she had to tell you everything and you-."

Anika, who was already feeling irritated, interrupted Nadine before she could finish. "So, spill. I wanna know all the dirty details."

"Well." she said, picking up a freshly washed dish from the rack. Her face turned crimson as she spoke. "He touched me."

Anika smirked, but kept silent as she rubbed the cloth against the next dish. After a few moments, she looked over her shoulder at Nadine, who set the dish down on the table and was staring into it like a lovesick pup.

"You look way too horny for just being touched. Come on, more details."

"I don't know. He ate me out, it was like in a porn."

Judging from the way the other girl blushed, Anika could only imagine how embarrassed she had been.

"Did you guys do it in the car?"

"No- we... um. It was outside." The girl's face paled.

"Where?"

"Uh. Just. Outside." Nadine looked over at Anika, who gave her a flat expression. "I bumped into him while I was walking here."

"Hmm. I know where you were." She gave Nadine a sad smile. "He goes to see them a lot. He doesn't take me with him because he hates seeing me cry."

"I'm sorry."

"It's not your fault. They died in an accident."

"I mean, for what happened at the..." the girl trailed off, unable to even tell Anika that she fucked her brother on their parents' grave.

"I guess you're not a virgin anymore."

"Oh, I am."

"What?" Anika nearly dropped the dish she was washing to stare in surprise at her.

"We just touched and stuff. Or really, he touched me. I promise, we didn't have sex on your parents' grave."

"Why wouldn't you? It honestly sounds really sexy." Anika pulled the plug and turned to face her friend with her hands on her hips.

"He stopped. He said if I still wanted it, I could go to him tonight." Nadine nearly dropped the plate she was drying. "Oops! That was close."

Anika began putting away the dishes Nadine set on the table. "After this, we can go shower. It will be just like at school, except more private."

10

DASHES OF EMPTINESS
Slade Darling

The girls would clean up and he could finally go get his rocks off. After nursing that wicked hard-on for so long, his dick was painfully sensitive. He dialed the code on the basement door and glanced back at the pair quickly, coveting them both. If he could fuck them, he would. That being said, he couldn't do anything to his precious sister, which is what made the girl in the basement such a convenient outlet. The brief engagement with his sister's friend had worn down his ability to control himself.

Once in the safety of his refuge, he leaned back against the door and closed his eyes, rubbing his hand on his joggers over his cock. It was instantly hard and ready for use. Good. The nasty cunt in the basement would have one more-...

Where the fuck was she?

His heart thundered in his ears, nearly making him vomit. Slade had to swallow several times to keep his dinner down.

The bitch wasn't tied to the bed where he left her. Wasn't that where he always left her? He left Anika tied to the bed every time he fucked her. No. It wasn't Anika. It was some whore he used as a substitute to prevent himself from acting on those deep, dark desires.

"Little whore?" he purred into the dimly lit basement. "I lied about letting you go. I planned to kill you all along. I just wanted to fuck your nasty hole until you liked it. I was gonna fuck you till you started begging me for more... and then I'd become bored... hmm. You are already boring me."

His eyes scanned the room from where he leaned back against the door at the top of the stairs. Maybe she was hiding under the stairs, squished behind the freezers or something. Maybe he left her locked in the freezer and forgot. He made that mistake a few times.

"If you come out... maybe I'll make your death painless. Or I'll lock you in the freezer again, and fuck you while you're nice and cold. I like the feeling of fucking them when they are cold. So, just as you're warming up, I'll stick you back in the freezer again. I'll do it on repeat until I take you out and learn that you froze to death."

Nothing. No sound, no begging. Maybe she found a weapon and was waiting somewhere down there for him. That could be fun. After being so gentle, he would love the opportunity to beat some little bitch into submission.

He hesitantly stepped forward, moving toward the railing so he could attempt to see closer to the freezers. His long fingers circled the wooden railing cautiously as he peered over the edge.

That was unexpected. The girl laid there in a disgruntled heap with wide eyes. Her gaze darted in every direction, but nothing else seemed to move. Her head sat at an unnatural angle, making it a miracle that she was even still alive.

The snort that came out of him was pure reflex, but an excited laugh followed it. He nearly felt giddy with the thought of what he planned to do to her. Slade flung himself down the stairs, skipping two or three at a time to reach the mangled doll quickly.

"Oh, you delicious little whore."

The only issue with the situation was that he couldn't remember breaking her neck. His cock was thundering with circulation, making it throb painfully with every movement.

Now that he stood next to her, he could see the sharp angle that her neck sat at and how her mouth lulled open with a trickle of drool hanging from it. Her toothless gums did nothing to prevent the string of saliva from leaking out. The girl laid in such a way that she could see the underside of the platform for the stairs and the freezer she'd inevitably end up in. Her legs and arms seemed spread out, as if awaiting his touch. Clearly, the girl could not move, which could both be fun and boring, depending on his mood.

"Blink once if you wanna fuck one last time," he taunted childishly.

Her nostrils flared as she closed her eyes tightly. A single tear rolled from the corner and down her temple.

"Close enough."

Holding off from fucking Anika's friend had been difficult, but he knew he had this doll waiting at home for him. He moved into place between her legs and pressed the ball of his foot against her pussy. He watched her face as he massaged small circles against the sensitive area. He contemplated removing his slipper so he could feel her clit swell from his touch, but Slade couldn't hold out any longer.

He shifted to his knees on the cement, then used one hand for balance and the other to direct his cock into her entrance. He gasped, groaning softly as he gently slid the tip of his cock into her entrance. Even though she was lying on the cold cement, her insides still felt delectably hot.

Nope. No more holding back.

Bucking his hips hard and fast, he slammed his entire length into the doll and instantly regretted it. She gasped as her body shifted from his movement. Her eyes rolled into the back of her head, and he felt her insides convulse around him a moment before her features relaxed.

"Bleghhh," he practically yelped, yanking his cock out of the whore. "Fuck!"

No one could hear his scream, because the only other person in the soundproof basement was a fucking corpse. The force behind his movement must have damaged her neck further because she clearly just died while he was balls deep inside her. It made him wonder for a moment if she'd been dead that entire time, and he hallucinated the rest.

"What's wrong with me?" he whimpered in a croak, shifting to sit on his ass and put his face in his hands.

His inner turmoil did nothing to dampen his cock's spirits. The massive erection between his thighs bounced joyfully. He wiped his tears with his palm before adjusting his joggers so that it no would longer hang out. For a split second, he considered trying to jack off, but the thought made him feel sick. Why wouldn't his damn hard-on go away? He was no longer even remotely close to feeling aroused. He pulled the waistband of his pants up to cover his dick.

Gathering his thoughts, Slade crawled to his feet. He pushed open the freezer and stared at the corpses of his previous victims. He pressed his hard dick against the side of the freezer, enjoying the feel of the cold metal seeping a chill through his pants.

There was a girl's hand sticking up high enough for her frozen fingers to touch the lid when it was closed. She was missing several nails and the blood trails that had rolled down her hand to her forearm had frozen. Her body laid beneath two others he had since she passed. He didn't even remember putting her in the freezer, but she died in there before he was ready to lose her. Not knowing why, Slade leaned forward and licked her icy fingertips. No taste. It wasn't what he expected. A moment of dizziness had him lean harder against the edge, clutching it with both hands.

He gave a sigh, wondering if he could make it the entire weekend before needing to go find another doll to replace the one with the broken neck and missing teeth. He crouched down and picked up the corpse from the ground. He chucked her into the freezer like the trash she was before slamming the lid shut.

Fuck. Slade stomped his way back up the stairs. For an instant, he considered punching the door, but thought better of it. Sade calmed himself before pressing the buttons on the keypad. The last thing he needed to do was freak the girls out.

After a few more minutes, he pressed the buttons and slipped out into the hall. His hard cock pressed against the front of his joggers, making it practically itch with a need for friction. Slade stared up and down the narrow space in search of the girls. Finding no one, he adjusted his dick so his tip could point upward. He stared down at the head poking out from the waistband of his pants before he shifted his shirt to cover it.

Judging from the sound of the running water, the girls were in the shower washing the chlorine and soil off. Tonight was definitely a wine night. It's possible Slade was simply pouting because his doll died before he had the chance to stalk the next. He didn't even remember killing her, but this wasn't the first time he didn't remember something like that. If the frequency of his blank spots, irritability and instability continued as they have, it certainly wouldn't be the last time.

Heaving a massive sigh, Slade pulled open the fridge door and grabbed the bottle of wine spritzer with approximately a cup missing from the contents. When had he even opened it? Anika pouted whenever he drank because her father loved to be intoxicated.

Tonight, she had a friend, and so did he; a liquid friend that will make everything feel alright.

Slade pulled out a wine glass from the cupboard above the fridge and tottered into the living room. He set the glass down and filled it before placing the bottle on the coffee table. As he sat down on the couch, he pulled out his phone and opened his camera app, curious to see what the girls were doing. Selecting current active cameras, he opted for the bathroom. The curtain was in the way, so he couldn't see the girls as they washed up. *Damn it.*

Adjusting the couch blankets, he hid his cock before taking his wine glass up in one hand. The bitter liquid sloshed into his mouth in a heavenly assortment of flavor and fizz. The wonderful drink came with the ability to escape the real world. The carbonation of the spritzer prickled his tongue, making the drink tastier and easier to handle.

Slade sighed in relief, knowing that he didn't have work the next day, though he was pretty sure he missed work earlier and would probably have to face a meeting with his supervisor.

He opened his camera app again, planning to spend some time enjoying old videos in the girl's change room at Anika's school, when he remembered she had pissed in his room the other day. Unless that all together was some sort of wishful hallucination. Either way, the whole thing was kind of hot.

His thumb flicked through the application links at lightning speed to find the correct location and time. His computer camera was the only one which could have picked up the situation. It took longer than he thought to find it, considering he had no ability to track time over the past several months. Having blank spots in his memories and hallucinations didn't help. Though he wasn't complaining about the ones with Anika fucking him, he wished those were real. His fear was that someday soon he would finally lose control and rape his precious little sister while thinking she was just a dream or one of his dolls. That thought made him feel sick.

While his mind stampeded in every direction, his fingers performed his fruitless search to find the clip of Anika in his room. Maybe the whole thing was a hallucination. The desperate search seemed to go on forever. Slade finished that glass of wine and had to refill it, not really noticing how fast it disappeared. He balanced the glass in one hand while using the other to search. Occasionally, he'd alternate between sips and massive swigs of the liquid.

"I'm such a lightweight," he murmured, realizing he was on his third glass and was already very dizzy.

Found it.

Turned out, his desperate search hadn't been for a memory of a hallucination. Which, ironically, had happened a few times. He'd remember something in so much detail, only to find nothing there, a video of him talking to himself, or fucking the couch cushions.

Anika walked into his space. She had the cutest little smile on her lips as she peered around his bedroom. Just watching her without her knowing he could see everything made him hornier.

She took a clip from her hair. The way it shimmered as it came loose and fluttered down about her shoulders made him circle his hard cock with his icy fingers. She had one of those adorable, mischievous smiles on her face as her pretty blue eyes scanned the room. She looked over her shoulder to glance out into the hallway, making a collarbone poke out from the V-line of her shirt. Slade moaned quietly, imagining that he was in his bed with her tip-toeing closer. He could almost smell her perfume and the faint scent of chlorine in the air. When Anika slipped the clip beneath his pillow, he sat there, feeling very confused.

He found that hair clip more than a week ago. He looked at the date on the corner of the page. Nearly a month. Where did the time go in there... Why didn't he notice anything sooner? What happened between then and the moment he finally thought to watch the video?

Certainly, he passed out on his bedroom floor only the other day. Wasn't that the same day as she entered his room? Slade felt a little sick, but the feeling subsided quickly when he watched his precious little sister sit down in his chair.

The little bitch was touching his shit! ... Oh dear.

Her perky little breasts became visible a mere moment before she tweaked her nipples. He watched with his mouth hanging open. It wasn't a dream. This was real... and she was beautiful. There was no way for him to know if it was a hallucination, and she'd surely done nothing like this before, at least where he might have caught her. He had one beloved video from her touching herself in her bed.

He kept the volume off, just in case the girls left the shower. He hated jacking off, but at that moment, it felt right. He kept his hand under the blanket and into his pants, where he stroked his massive, throbbing cock. Watching her pull her bottom lip into her mouth made a small trickle of cum spill out, dampening the front of his jogging pants.

He could no longer cope with the restraining pull from the waistband of his pants, so he pushed it down and freed his dick. Even the blanket felt like too much weight, but if the girls came into the room, he didn't want them to get an eyeful of his cock and freak out. As Anika climaxed in the video, so did he. Slade came so hard that his eyes rolled back into his head and hot cum splattered his stomach, dribbling across his ribs and onto the couch.

He trembled for a moment before relaxing and closing his eyes. So much had built up in such a short amount of time. The phone rested on his palm at his side and his other hand kept his cock warm, though it was still a throbbing mass.

Why? Why was he always so hard? Even with his cock still pounding with a desperate need for interaction, Slade felt himself slowly drifting to sleep, unable to keep his eyes open any longer.

11

GIRL TIME
Anika Darling

The girls headed to the bathroom as soon as they finished with the dishes. She quickly placed Nadine's luggage in her room and fetched her pajamas from her drawers while the other girl dug around in her book bag.

"That's all that happened?" Anika questioned, sounding disappointed.

"Yeah, but he said I can go to him later tonight. I think I'm gonna do it. I really want to lose my virginity and I don't care what the circumstances are."

"Be careful what you wish for," Anika teased, then followed up with, "Just be happy Slade was gentle with you."

"I can't even picture him being rough. He was so sweet. It was like every touch had the sole purpose of pleasing me. He was amazing and made me feel better than I could ever imagine."

She turned to face the other girl with raised eyebrows. The thought that this girl could fall in love with Slade made Anika want to vomit. He was *her* brother. He was her everything. They needed each other, and no one could replace the bond between them. Their life force was connected!

She made herself take a calming breath. He would never fall in love with this skinny, breastless airhead and abandon her... would he? That she felt so insecure about it annoyed her.

Her brother was all kinds of messed up, but surely things would find balance soon.

"Are you in love with him?"

"What?! Ewe. I don't love anyone."

"Don't 'ewe' my brother. Especially not when you're planning to fuck him."

"I was ewe-ing the idea of being in love, that's all." Nadine corrected, standing with her pajamas in her hand.

"Oh! Your pajamas are so cute! Slade makes me wear pant suit pajamas. Can we trade? I'd love to wear something so slinky and sexy."

"What? No." Nadine giggled. "It's not even mine. I borrowed it."

"From who? Your mom?" Anika questioned, leading the way into the hall and down toward the bathroom.

"Nooo..." Nadine's cheeks were on fire as she responded. "Someone else."

"Oh. Torren." Anika teased, grinning over her shoulder as she stepped onto the cold tile bathroom floor.

When Nadine's face turned a deep crimson, she couldn't help raising an eyebrow. The other girl was such an easy target to taunt that it was almost boring... almost.

"Yes." Nadine sighed and closed the door behind them as if she thought it would stop any prying eyes. "This whole thing was her idea. She knows how bad I wanna lose my virginity. She said Slade fucked her about a year ago and it was the best she's ever had... which is saying a lot, considering the rumors about her."

"She definitely has enough experience to talk." Anika chuckled, turning on the faucet.

She gave the spraying water a moment to warm up while she peeled off her uniform. Once naked, she bent over and stuck her hand into the flow. The warm water gushed across her icy fingers.

Looking over her shoulder at Nadine as the smaller woman stripped, Anika noticed something out of place. "Your ass is all scratched up."

"That's from the-" her cheeks heated, and she shook her head.

"Common, you know you wanna tell me."

"I feel bad because they were your parents, too."

Anika snorted far louder than she meant to. She pulled the curtain all the way around the tub to ensure that wherever her brother's camera was, it couldn't see into the area.

"You can make it up to me," Anika teased with a playful wink over her shoulder as she stepped into the bathtub.

"He sat me on the tombstone..." she whispered like she was testing the metaphorical waters... when Anika giggled, she continued, "he licked me down there until I came. I had my first serious orgasm. My whole body tingled!"

When she fluttered her fingers in the air, Nadine joined her in the shower. "Oh! It's a little chilly!"

Anika enjoyed watching Nadine's body react to the chill in the water. It was very different without the swimsuit hiding the goosebumps and hardened nipples. She giggled and lightly flicked one of Nadine's nipples. The other girl gasped, covering them with her palms. Her brows drew down as she turned sideways and stepped away so the water splattered the bottom half of her face.

"Look how sensitive they are!" Anika announced excitedly, doing her best to make Nadine feel comfortable as she exploited her body.

"It's embarrassing." Nadine whined irritatingly.

Anika felt her demeanor change. Her mask of friendly playfulness quickly vanished, being replaced by the emotionless expression that came naturally to her. She stepped closer, watching as Nadine inched to the edge of the tub until her calf pressed against the side. Anika had to tilt her head to the side to keep the showering water from splattering her face. It hit her shoulder

"What's wrong? You're freaking me out." The stupid girl looked like she was on the verge of tears.

"I know Torren told you the whole deal. She wouldn't leave the important parts out." Anika's voice was dangerously low.

Nadine's eyes widened in surprise. "I thought she was joking, you know, like pulling my leg."

"You knew she wasn't." Anika tilted her head to the side to stop the water from splashing on her face as she advanced closer to the shorter girl.

"I- I don't know if I can do what you want."

"You don't have to do anything, just like with Slade."

"How do you know I didn't do anything?"

Anika gave the girl a playful smile, which didn't touch her eyes. The mask was already gone. There was no point in putting in the effort to fully return it. Her hand came up to gently cup the quivering girl's cheek.

"It's okay. It's better with a woman anyway, and I won't do anything he didn't do, so behave yourself."

Her free hand circled Nadine's wrist to lead her back into the flow of the water. It seemed every small step was agonizing for the other girl. Once beneath the spray, water rebounded off Nadine, sprinkling Anika's face. With the water bordering on cool, the girls' nipples became painfully hard once more.

Anika found herself pleasantly surprised by how much she enjoyed pinching both her hard nipple and Nadine's at the same time. It was as if she could share that state of pleasure with another person. The other girl whimpered quietly, becoming very tense. Maybe she liked it, though it was possible the girl was so tense from anxiety.

Anika moved to crouch down in front of Nadine. It was a test to gauge the girl's reaction. Unfortunately, this little bitch wasn't nearly as cooperative as Torren had been. Nadine practically yelped and moved her hands to cover her hairless pussy.

Instead of touching or licking her, Anika reached behind the girl and adjusted the faucet to make the water cold. As Anika stood, Nadine gasped and stepped forward, bumping right into her.

"Now you leap into my arms?"

"N-no. The water. It's too cold!"

"This is nothing. I shower in way colder water than this to train for swimming. You can handle this."

The stupid girl was already shivering and shaking her head. Anika held Nadine against her body, forcing the smaller swimmer to remain in the stream of icy water.

"As soon as I'm done, we can enjoy our hot shower."

"Oh-Okay," Nadine agreed, trembling from the cold. Within moments, her teeth were chattering. "Go ahead. Touch me."

She pulled Nadine's painfully erect nipple into her mouth, warming the sensitive flesh with her tongue. The other girl gasped and moved her hands to push gently against Anika's shoulders, but it didn't slow her down. She swirled her tongue in circles around the nipple and allowed her teeth to graze the puffy flesh. Sucking lightly, she used her lips to pinch it tightly while flicking her tongue at the underside. She held on hard and pulled her face away, so the suction made a soft popping noise as Nadine's nipple broke free of her vacuous mouth.

Ignoring the water splattering on her face, she moved across to the other nipple while replacing her mouth with her fingers. She lightly pinched and twisted that tiny nipple, while wondering if she was better at this sexual play than Slade was.

Nadine whimpered loudly, but instead of sitting back and enjoying the attention like Torren did, her hands continued to apply pressure on Anika's shoulders, as if pushing her away. It was annoying her far more than it should have. She dragged her teeth a little harder than necessary across the girl's areola.

"Owe!" she stepped back, making the stream of water spray over her shoulder and hit Anika in the face.

Stepping back, Anika wiped the water from her eyes.

"What the hell?" she snarled, glaring at the girl.

"I'm sorry, you hurt me. You said you would do what he did, but he never hurt me."

"And I'm sure you never pushed him away." Anika snapped a quick retort, not meaning to come across as aggressive as she did.

She moved forward, but when Nadine flinched and closed her eyes, Anika simply reached past her to adjust the temperature. She made the water far warmer than she liked. Now that the other girl was so uncomfortable, she needed to make her feel secure.

"I'm sorry." Anika whispered and pulled Nadine into the flow of warm water. "Let me help you feel better."

Anika wrapped her arms around the shorter girl, holding her close so their bodies twined together. The water splattered Nadine's backside and Anika's face, but she closed her eyes and used her body to cocoon the smaller girl. She brought a hand back and stroked the back of Nadine's head, while lightly kissing her temple.

"I'm sorry." Nadine whispered. "I'm just scared."

"I just want us to feel good."

"I know." The girl's mumble into Anika's chest was a breath of warm air, making her more aroused.

Her hands roamed the other girl's body, finding every crevasse and curve, only to exploit it and move on. She leaned down, pressing her lips to Nadine's collar. Anika licked at the water dribbling across the other girl's skin, enjoying the clean taste it gave her. Her fingers cupped the girl's small behind. *Such a tiny ass for a swimmer.*

Trailing those kisses, licks and nips up Nadine's neck to distract her, Anika let her fingers maneuver their way to the short girl's pussy. She carefully rubbed the lips, not entering until she was sure it wouldn't startle her.

She pulled away to stare down into Nadine's shimmering eyes. Her cheeks were flushed with heat and arousal as the room filled with steam.

"Kiss me." Anika's voice practically purred.

Nadine's glazed eyes seemed especially sleepy when she blinked cluelessly, as if lost in a daze. Anika planted her lips firmly on Nadine's before drawing the girl's plump bottom lip into her mouth and nipping lightly before sucking. She ran her tongue along the lip before releasing it and resuming the kiss with far more tenderness.

Her finger finally slipped inside that fiery slit to find Nadine's taunt clit desperately waiting for attention. When she rubbed small circles around the nub, the smaller swimmer whimpered into her mouth. Which, in all honesty, added flavor to the unemotional kiss. Anika moved her hand from Nadine's nipple to rest on her throat, in a display of dominance to ensure her full control. She could feel the blood pulsing beneath her fingers as the girl came so much closer to orgasm.

Anika crept her body down, kissing a trail along the wet flesh while making her way to Nadine's pussy.

"Wait!" Nadine gasped, flinching away from Anika once again.

Quickly becoming irritated, Anika tilted her head back to glare up at the other girl as water splattered her face.

She squinted to see through the mist as she spoke. "I get to do to you, whatever *he* did to you. That's the deal."

"But I want *him* to take my virginity. I don't want to have sex with you."

Anika's eyes narrowed. Her knees were already hurting from the metal bottom of the tub. It took every bit of acting skill she had to keep her mask and appear calm and comforting.

"I want you to let me lick it because it looks so delicious. And then, right after, you have my blessing to lose your virginity."

"And I won't have to fuck you?"

"And you won't have to fuck me."

"Okay." Nadine nodded, looking more confident in her decision.

Anika didn't need more invitations than that. She grabbed Nadine's ass to hold her in place and practically slammed her face into that beautiful pussy. Her tongue plowed between those bald lips and claimed that pulsating clit with a desperate need that only eating Nadine out in that moment could satiate.

"OH FUCK!" Nadine yelped loudly as her legs immediately began twitching wildly.

The only thing holding her up was Anika's rough grip on her ass, but that was supposed to be mild support to keep the other swimmer positioned right. Her tongue went from fast strokes to slow circles, basking in the sweet flavor of the other girl's pussy. Nadine moaned loudly, stepping back, but catching a tight grip on the shower curtain. The shift forced Anika to follow her into the stream of water. Anika moaned, closing her eyes as water splattered her face. Nadine nearly lost her balance again and placed her other hand on the wall as she shifted positions, attempting to spread her thighs.

"Fuck, sit on the side of the tub."

"I'm uh. I'm dizzy."

"Then sit the fuck down."

"Okay."

Anika securely gripped Nadine's arm to help her shift to the back end of the tub. This way, the water would hit Anika's back and she'd have plenty of room to kneel and pleasure her friend. Once Nadine sat comfortably on the side of the tub with her hands clutching the curtain around her like a cape, Anika buried her face into Nadine's pussy as if making the other girl climax was her duty.

Nadine gasped loudly, with her hands releasing the curtain to tangle her fingers in Anika's hair.

"Oh, my- go... My head. The world is spinning."

Anika felt the girl's strong swimmer's legs tense and applied pressure to both sides of her head, trapping her there. Caged as she was, it didn't slow her steadfast attack on the delicious clitoris dancing with her tongue.

"I'm cumming. Oh my–Anika. You're... wow. I'm. I feel like I'm gonna faint. Fuck."

12

SWEET WILD VIRGIN
Slade Darling

The head-buzz from his drink and post orgasmic goodness sent Slade spiraling into a deep slumber. There was a faint sound of moaning in the distance. The sound made his hard cock throb beneath his hand.

After recent events, he felt exceptionally unfulfilled. So, it only made sense that his dreams would be of an extremely sexual nature. In this sleeping state, he felt just as weak and helpless as any other. His limbs didn't want to cooperate and rested where he left them, with a numb tingling echoing up through them.

There was something warm touching his lips. As he struggled to open his eyes, he found the world spun around him. It made seeing the dimly lit room impossible.

"Come on. I know you want it," he heard a female voice whimper as something squished against his mouth. "Or you wouldn't be so hard."

Within a deep breath, he could practically taste the pussy pressing to his lips. The sweet and earthy scent seemed to twine with the floral aroma of body wash. He moaned and instinctively opened his mouth to take temptation upon his tongue. From the moisture on his face, he wondered how long that pussy had rubbed on him. He didn't even have the strength to lift his head from the backrest of the couch.

He promised Anika's friend that he would pleasure her, but never expected this kind of invitation. Her clit was already a pulsating, swollen nub, demanding attention as she ground herself against him. The hem of her silky nightgown tickled his forehead when she released her hold on it. The slim, small swimmer arched her back to bask in his sudden participation.

It took him far too long to realize that the moaning he heard came from two sources. One had her pussy pressed to his face, and the other came from his phone, which rested on the cushion next to him. Somehow, the audio increased, so Anika's soft, gasping moans from the video of her touching herself echoed in the large room.

He reached for the phone with plans to silence the delightful sounds. Her foot got there first. She pushed the phone out of his reach. No! If this dumb girl told people about the video, it would destroy the image he'd worked so hard to build for them.

"Leave it. It turns me on."

What a vivacious young woman! He moaned, becoming so excited by the mere thought of Nadine and him fucking while listening to the audio of Anika masturbating that he nearly reached completion on his own. His hand moved to massage his cock, squeezing tightly at the base, hoping to halt his oncoming orgasm. His other hand grabbed her ankle and slid up that slim but muscular swimmer's leg.

He could even smell the faintest of chlorine on her, which was a perfect catalyst to help him imagine it was Anika. No amount of perfume or soap could wash away the chlorine. It was one of the best parts of sleeping with his sister's teammates. They all smelled the same as she did.

'Anika. I love you. I need you.' he thought desperately while eating out her little friend.

He could hardly open his eyes, but when Slade squinted, he numbly realized she covered him with the hem of her nightie. The darkly shadowed curves of her taut core and small breasts were barely visible. He closed his eyes and began rubbing his tongue against that delicious little clit.

"I'm so happy you woke up." the young woman gave a throaty whimper, twining her icy fingers through his dark hair. "I knew you would, eventually."

She moaned again, arching her back as she rolled her hips, practically fucking his face. He reciprocated by pushing his tongue hard against her before swirling around her clit.

Finally regaining some strength, he flexed his right hand open and closed while his other lightly massaged his cock. He moved his freehand to her ankle. His fingers slid their way up the back of her leg, delicately trailing over the back of her knees. She whimpered, almost giggling, and her knees bent, pushing into the backrest of the couch to escape his touch.

The girl was ticklish. How cute. He moved both his hands to her ass and grabbed it, assisting her to ride his face with more force.

"I'm going to cum!" she shrieked before her hips bucked wildly, trying to escape the hypersensitivity of her overstimulated clitoris.

He held her tight, forcing her through the overwhelming tornado of agonizing pleasure. While her clit built in stiffness against his tongue, he slowed his movements. He kept her firmly in place as he eased her through the lingering waves of sensitivity. It started in barely a trickle, but he shifted her forward so his nose rubbed her clit as he sucked her tight hole, drinking as much of her cum as he could. Regardless of how hard he tried, when the rush came forth, cum spilled from the corners of his mouth, rolling down his body. It dampened his shirt, but he paid it no mind.

"That was amazing. You are... wow!"

Her praises made his skin tingle with excitement. He would take this little woman's virginity and turn her into a whore! Knowing what was to come made his dick throb painfully. Her virgin pussy was going to wrap tightly around his cock. He'd make her bleed for him and then beg for more. Fuck, he forgot condoms!

Her pussy slid down his chin until it rested on his chest. He could feel the heat of it through his wet shirt. She slowly slid the wet piece of heaven down his torso, as if coating him with her desire. He moaned out before interrupting himself.

"Condom. Nadine."

"No need for protection," she purred, pausing with her pussy pressing on his stomach and her nightgown held over his head.

His excitement was barely containable. She was playing perfectly into his most recent fantasies. He'd never actually done it without a condom, aside from that tiny moment downstairs when the whore died while he put it in. That was something he didn't plan to relive any time soon.

His hands slid up her sides, enjoying that curvature where her hips met her waistline.

She wiggled atop him, giggling softly before grabbing his wrists and moving his hands beneath the dress. The naughty girl led him right to her breasts. She leaned forward, pressing her nipple to his lips, encouraging him to take action. He used one hand to pinch a nipple, while his mouth opened and accepted her other. His free hand slid back down to her ass, offering support. After all, she was squatting with her pussy pressed against him to make sure he could enjoy her tits.

"Nadine, you're so adventurous this time." He mumbled, licked her nipple, then continued, "I take it our meeting in the park encouraged this?"

She giggled softly before standing. Her thigh length tight gown held firm around his head, so all he could see was her navel, then her pussy. The moment he moved his face forward to claim that wonder piece of paradise, the little bitch turned away. The ass it was then. He moved his face forward but had to stop when she shifted positions to kneel. His cock pressed against her entrance as she reverse-cowgirl'd him. With nimble fingers, he traced the curves in her wonderful, tiny body as the head of his cock pushed into her tight hole.

"Oh fuck." He groaned, blinking as the nightgown slipped off his head, exposing the dark room around him.

The only light sources were the shimmering moonlight from the bay window and the dim glow from the video of Anika feeling herself up, which apparently was being played on repeat. It allowed him to see basic shapes in the room, but any details were impossible to distinguish.

His eyes adjusted to the dark, but he was way more intoxicated than the three or four glasses of wine should have allowed. The room spun around him until his eyes landed on his dear sister sitting on a chair in the corner. Slade blinked several times, trying to figure out if she was a hallucination or if maybe he really was dreaming. *Why would Anika stay there watching this?!*

She sat stiffly, with her arms on the rests of the wooden kitchen chair. She wiggled and squirmed, moaning loudly.

"Oh, you shouldn't be seeing this." He called to her before snapping at Nadine. "Get off me."

He placed his hands against the girl's back, wanting to push her, but the pleasure from her pussy enclosing around the tip of his cock sent a ripple of pleasure across his body.

"She wants to watch. She dreams about fucking you. Losing her virginity to you." the girl atop him purred as his cock slipped all the way into her entrance. "Oh yes. It feels so good."

His hands trailed up and down the sides of the woman who rode him. She started slowly, but quickly picked up the pace. His fingers squeezed the girl, but he didn't have the physical strength to push her off him.

"I can't fuck you, sweet girl." He whimpered between gasps.

Slade couldn't pull his eyes from Anika's while Nadine pounded herself atop him so hard he was sure the suction of her insides was about to rip his dick off.

"Anika." He moaned her name and watched as she closed her eyes. "I love you. Please, don't be mad at me for fucking your friend."

She opened her eyes and stared at him with her eyebrows drawn down over them.

"Can I make your friend cum? I can, right? You'd like it if she came?" he reached around as he spoke, hooking his arm under her leg as he moved in search of her clit. "Cum, little whore. Cum for my sister."

He no longer cared about it being Anika's friend atop him. She was watching; she wanted him to do it. His fingers massaged the girl's clit, feeling her pussy clench and tighten around him. Enough was enough. He wanted her to make a mess. He desperately wanted Anika to see how he could bring pleasure to a woman's body. Slade hooked his other forearm beneath the little swimmer's other leg and lifted her until only his tip remained inside. With the flats of his fingers pressing against her clit, attempting to continue stimulating the area, he began thrusting himself inside her. Anchoring his shoulders against the back of the couch, and the balls of his feet against the carpeted floor, he pounded his flesh unrelentingly into the hole she presented him with.

His rapture was so great that she screamed out, but he didn't care if it was from pain or pleasure. He finally lost his self-control.

"Losing your virginity is supposed to hurt, but you have deprived me of that."

He snarled, landing her back down onto his cock before raising her so much that he slipped out. Slade sat up, attempting to maneuver his cock so it would slip back in. Instead, his dick tried to penetrate her other virgin hole. That would ensure losing her virginity was something she'd never forget.

As the tip pressed against her tight anus, the girl screamed and thrashed around so hard he nearly dropped her.

"Not my ass. You fucking idiot!" the girl shrieked, but his attention was on the shadowed girl seated in the chair at the corner of the room.

That entrance wasn't something he considered using until his eyes met Anika's. Her eyes lit up with glee, though the rest of her features didn't change. He realized now; she wanted him to hurt Nadine. If Anika liked it, then whatever the other girl wanted was obsolete. Slade quickly stood, dragging the girl by her hair as he clumsily maneuvered in the dark around the couch to bend her over its backside.

"What the fuck are you doing?! Let me go!" She screamed, clawing at his hand tangled in her hair. "NO!"

He bent her over the couch and reached forward, covering her mouth. Her relentless shrieking made his head pound. The throbbing practically blinded him, forcing his eyes shut to cope. Her slobber made his hand slick when she tried to use her tongue to force his hand to move. If she wanted it that way, he would comply.

In a moment of fury and excitement, his hands shifted to the sides of her neck, blocking the air and blood flow. His icy fingers curled around her throat, using it for leverage as he slammed his cock balls deep into her tight little asshole. It shocked him when she managed to get a scream out while he strangled her.

The swimmer's hands went from clawing at his fingers to balling them into tight fights and moved to press against him in a feeble attempt to stop him from moving. It didn't even phase him. Slade began moving, slamming his pelvis against her ass as he took her tiny little hole and claimed it as his own.

When her screams subsided and she went limp, he wondered if she had fallen unconscious. He released her throat and snatched up a solid grip on her hair. Slade gave her a good shake, so she started awake and her ass tightening around his cock. A small amount of blood trickled down, which became lubricant for his savage pulverization on her asshole. She didn't even fight, simply wept, which suited him all the better.

"We are gonna keep you and I'm gonna fuck you all the damn time. I've got one question." He slowed his movements as he edged closer to cumming. "If your last pill was today, and I cum inside you now, will you be pregnant tomorrow?"

As if performing for an ultimate finale, he pulled his cock out and rammed it into her pussy, before letting himself explode. He moaned, pulling out a bit and pushing it back in as every ounce of seamen he had surged from the tip of his cock into the woman's depths. He finished, using up every ounce of strength he had.

The universe spun around him and his cock slipped out, still, miraculously hard, as he collapsed to the ground. His blurry vision spun the room around him one last time as he lost consciousness.

13

NO ESCAPING THE PAST
Anika Darling

That night was the toughest sleep she'd had in years. The only thing she could recollect from her nightmare was her parents fighting.

Those dreams were normal, considering that was their relationship's default mode, until one day, Daddy stopped arguing. He stopped doing anything wrong and just did whatever Mommy wanted. For a while, life improved after that change, but it was simply the calm before the storm.

Her eyes ripped open in a panic. The sound of her parent's voices screaming at each other echoed and faded into memory.

Anika slowly sat up, looking at the fat little stuffed animal she was hugging in her sleep. She practically strangled the damn piggy teddy in her search for comfort. Pigs freaked her out, yet that one stuffy was her favorite out of all of them. Pigs eat anything. ANYTHING.

She stumbled from her room with bags under her eyes and her hair in a messy bun on the side of her head.

She drank the rest of Slade's wine spritzer after he fainted like a damn sissy boy. He was so wasted that he would think he drank it all himself.

Who would believe his angelic little sister did?

Everything hurt. She felt like she got hit by a truck. And then the fucker backed over her... two or three times. She had a headache and felt like every cell in her body was dying.

Chances are, Slade would be amid another mental lapse and the best thing for her to do would be to escape the house for a bit while he got his head on straight.

It didn't take her too long to finish taking care of herself in the bathroom. Before leaving the room, she stared in the mirror, noting her meticulously brushed hair and flawlessly maintained skin.

Her startling blue eyes were glassy with dark bags beneath them and she had a slight bruise on her left cheek just under her temple. This wouldn't do. Hopefully, no one noticed the damage to her cheek.

Anika pressed her palms against her eyes and rubbed hard. She pulled away to check the difference in color before doing it two more times. When her hands pulled away the third time, her lips curled into the smallest of smiles. Perfection. Her eyes were red rimmed and raw from the rubbing, making them bloodshot, as if she'd been crying.

Anika went back to her room and grabbed her spare swimsuit, which was this gaudy pink and purple thing. She liked the black suits that the school provided the swim team with. Slade dressed her like a little girl, as if reminding himself she was his sweet little sister. She held the bejeweled swimwear up to examine, mentally cringed from the pain shooting down her arms.

She packed her spare swim bag, knowing Slade hadn't washed her other one. When did he have time during his little bender the night before? Alcohol always makes it worse when he snaps like that. There's nothing she could do but wait until he stopped. It was a relief when he fainted.

When she was ready to go, she tiptoed down the hallway. Next to the basement door, she could see clearly into the living room and kitchen simultaneously. The space was large and open- almost inviting. There he rested, behind the couch on the floor, right where she left him.

"Slade?" she cautiously called to him, not daring to go closer.

Having made that mistake before, she learned the lesson. She could still feel his hands around her throat from when she woke him and he lashed out, strangling her. Luckily, he didn't remember the attack, or he'd never get over the guilt.

"Slade!"

Nothing. The fucker didn't even twitch.

Marching past him, she went to the door, her hand rested on the handle, and she opened it. Last time he passed out in the living room like that, he only woke when she tried to sneak out. He flipped out about safety and security. It was actually quite terrifying. Her stomach growled quietly, but she ignored the rumbling. She hated eating before swimming. Waiting there with the door open made her feel as if she was going to get caught doing something she shouldn't.

"Slade!"

This was getting ridiculous. Every time she yelled his name, her whole body clenched painfully. She just wanted to stretch her sore muscles, then go swimming.

"Mommy, no!" she hissed, and he finally startled awake with a twitch.

"Anika!" he yelped groggily, slowly peeling himself up from the floor.

He blinked, tilting his head from side to side before twisting around to find her in front of the door. His brows furrowed and jaw clenched in anger before his eyes narrowed.

"What the fuck are you doing?" he snapped at her, making her flinch.

"I was trying to see-," she sniffled, "if I can go visit mommy and daddy."

She quivered her chin, and he shifted to sitting on his ass with his hands, finally adjusting his crotch to hide his limp dick. He was facing away from her, and probably thought she didn't notice it hanging out above the waistband of his pants. His back was to her, and he twisted his upper body so his gaze could meet hers.

"Were you crying?"

Good, the appearance of reddening around her eyes made him think she had wept and threw him off enough that he didn't fly into a rage. She drew her bottom lip into her mouth and bit down on it before shaking her head slightly.

"Tell me!" He roared, making her splitting headache so much worse.

In a rapid spew of words, she recited the speech she'd created as fast as she could. "I had a nightmare about mommy and daddy, so I want to go to see them and then- then I thought we could go to the pool. I can meet you at the pool at two, so you don't have to go with me to the–the- where mommy and daddy are."

She made a point of panting lightly, with a quivering jaw for good measure. Her arms wrapped around herself as if in comfort, but even that motion hurt, making her close her eyes tightly. They even watered slightly from the pain. Anika always made a point of crying hard when they went to the grave together, knowing Slade couldn't handle her tears. So, her only real escape from him was to claim she was going to see those dead assholes.

"Two?" he repeated, taking far too long to process everything.

Slade suddenly stood and moved toward her. She flinched away from him in a panic, unsure of what he was going to do. The day after a mental break, he could be extremely volatile, and she didn't want to risk him losing control and attacking her.

"Don't you want a hug goodbye?" he questioned with furrowed eyebrows.

His question eased the bubble of panic that built up in her gut.

"Yes, please. I would love a hug from you." She wrapped her arms around his waist and buried her face in his chest.

Even after drinking and vomiting on the floor in his sleep, he still smelled so good. Beneath the scent of alcohol, puke and whatever else, he smelled like Slade. His soaps and colognes wafted in the air around him like a delicious cloak. She clutched at the back of his shirt, trying to pull him harder against her.

"I love you, Slade," she whimpered against his chest.

His cool lips pressed to the top of her head. "I love you too, my dear, sweet little sister."

She stood there, enjoying the feel of him for as long as he continued to hold her. Finally, he let go and stepped away.

"Where's your friend?"

"Last night... she seemed really freaked out," she carefully muttered, not wanting to set him off. "She said something about losing her virginity and the pain." Every word she spoke was true.

"Oh. Sorry, sweety."

His brows drew down in confusion and he shook his head

slowly, as if he had little to no recollection from the night before. Anika shrugged, stepping away from Slade, and tilted her head to the side.

"I didn't like her much, anyway."

The bitch beat her in the swim meet the day before. She got what she deserved. Anika pushed some loose strands of hair behind her shoulder and flinched.

"What's wrong?"

"Period cramps," she lied, knowing she hadn't had a period in months, but she wasn't about to tell him that.

He was so out of his mind that she didn't even feel the need to fake it and put tampons in the garbage. Slade didn't really notice much of anything lately.

He slowly nodded. "Okay. No swimming until I get to the pool to watch over you, right?"

"Of course not."

He patted the top of her head before reaching past her to push the door open. This was her stoic, powerful brother. She missed him while he was gone.

Once she was outside, he closed the door behind her. Anika made her way to the school, not bothering with going to the graveyard. She broke into the pool building the same way she used to when the location had been a hotel. After the school burned down, the town bought the hotel over and turned it into a new educational institution with a pool and everything. The school burning down was the best thing that could have happened to this town, as far as Anika was concerned.

Her plan was to swim, and when he was due to arrive, she'd go into the change room, jump in the shower and act like she had just prepared for swimming. She held her bladder for the entire morning, just to piss in the pool. For her, it felt like a way to mark her territory. Swimming was the only thing that was truly hers.

Anika stripped herself of her clothes in the main swimming area, not caring about the security cameras. If there was a guard, and he reported her after all this time, she'd point out that she'd been doing this for years and swimming nude the entire time. She'd destroy his life and have him named a pervert for watching her. Especially considering that she had only just turned eighteen. She was fourteen the first time she broke in and swam naked, trying to feel closer to the water.

The thought of swimming naked aroused her more than she'd admit. The way the water could touch every fiber of skin and enter her crevasses freely. Instead of diving in, she opted for the ladder for a slow descent into the chilly liquid. Her whole body was too tired and in far too much pain to risk jumping in.

Anika simply allowed herself to enjoy the water and silence. Finally, fully immersed, she laid back and let herself float, hovering in the water as she rested. There was nothing but her, the water and the echo of her soft breaths in the grand open space.

14

SICK SENSE OF HUMOR
Slade Darling

The memories of the previous night would float into his thoughts and quickly recede, as if his own mind didn't want him to remember what happened. With his arms wrapped around his precious sister, he found her smell to be too mesmerizing. Letting go would be impossible. He pressed his lips to the top of her head and breathed deep, wishing he could bottle that scent and stay like that for eternity.

Even though she hadn't been in the pool since the day before, the chemicals still clung to her skin and hair as if it was a part of her. The girl's tiny frame practically trembled between his arms when he gave her a light squeeze. He cocooned her with his body, praying desperately not to have to release her.

Unfortunately, he had no choice but to pull away and stare down into her beautiful blue eyes. She looked... suspicious? Maybe she was finally catching onto the fact that he had some mental health issues. Hopefully, she knew he would never hurt her.

"I love you, Slade," she whimpered, with the heat of her breath warming his chest through his shirt.

Pressing his lips to the top of her head, he took another deep breath, enjoying the smell and feel of her, "I love you too," he nearly choked on the words. "My dear, sweet little sister."

He couldn't understand why he was feeling so choked up. It was becoming nearly painful to breathe, and tears burned his eyes. He gave her one last squeeze before releasing her and stepping away. Using thoughts of the other girl to take the chance and look around the room. He hoped to avoid her noticing how weak he really was.

"Where's your friend?"

"Last night... she seemed really freaked out," she muttered, almost impossible to hear as her voice cracked over the words. "She said something about losing her virginity and the pain."

The guilt was overwhelming, but he could barely remember what happened the previous night. Did he fuck her? Did he take her virginity? If it hurt, then it was possible that the girl was going to cause them issues. His jaw locked in a moment of rage, which he quickly suppressed, knowing Anika was closely watching.

"Oh. Sorry, sweety," he forced out an apology, hoping it would soothe any irritation she might have over the previous night.

Did he actually fuck the girl? And if he did, why couldn't he remember?! His brows drew down in confusion and he shook his head slowly.

Anika shrugged, stepping away from Slade, and tilted her head to the side. He cocked an eyebrow, hoping she wasn't cross with him for something he simply couldn't remember.

"I didn't like her much, anyway."

Relief flooded him, even though she looked pretty pissed off. The simple fact that she wasn't mad at him was enough to soothe him. She looked so beautiful, tilting her head to the side while her hair circled her pretty face. Anika pushed some loose strands of hair behind her shoulder and flinched.

"What's wrong?"

"Period cramps," she told him, making him mentally flinch back from the conversation.

Nope. That was not a discussion he wished to pursue. That she was a woman was not something he was comfortable facing. She was still his little baby sister. As long as she wasn't a woman, he could contend with not laying a hand on her. He had to keep that thought in the forefront of his mind. She was just a sweet little girl... or he would destroy the family they built together.

"Okay. No swimming until I get to the pool to watch over you, right?"

The thought of her drowning made him feel sick and dizzy. If he wasn't there that day so many years ago, she would have died alongside their parents.

"Of course not."

He patted the top of her head before reaching past her to push the door open. His heart thrummed so hard that his chest ached. She needed to leave quickly, or he'd break down in front of her. He felt as if his mind was abandoning him. It was best that she left. Between the smell of her and his sense of sanity waning, he worried what he would do to her.

The moment she set foot outside, Slade became overwhelmed with his emotions. He closed the door and locked it before turning to lean back against it while panting heavily. Slade tightly closed his eyes, but tears leaked out anyway, gushing from their confines behind his eyelids to trickle down his cheeks. Without thinking, he screamed. It was a wordless sound of agony and rage that ripped its way from the depths of his soul.

When the air ran out, he took another deep breath and set his voice free again. This happened on repeat until his vocals broke and he noiselessly shrieked. When he could do that no more, he wept, grabbing his head in his hands and letting his legs gave way so he could slide down the door to the floor. An obnoxious noise though grit teeth followed every inhale as the air expressed from his lungs. While it escaped while he struggled and failed to control his breathing.

Immediately following the unstable release of anguish, Slade's mind was overcome by a numb rage. It wasn't as if he thought about destroying everything. He felt he needed to be physical, and he simply moved anything in his way... violently. A deep bellow rolled from his chest as he flung himself to his feet. Maddened eyes darted around a relatively empty house in search of a target for his rage. He marched into the living room, getting flashbacks of violently tearing into Nadine's ass.

"Fuck!" he hissed before shrieking, "FUCK!

He crouched down, grabbing the back of the couch. A memory flashed in his mind where he used that piece of furniture to hold his sister's friend steady while he basically raped her. She wasn't supposed to become like one of his victims. The little bitch would likely cry at her parents about what he did and destroy their lives! He slipped his hands under the couch and stood, throwing the fucking thing across the room, hitting the tv in the far corner. Slade leaned over and puked, retching loudly as alcohol and stomach acid burned its way up his throat, splattering the hardwood floor.

With the couch very much gone, his eyes darted to the empty bottle standing on the glass table. He grabbed it by the neck and raised it over his head to whip it through the entrance that led to the kitchen area and froze.

There was a chair blocking the wide entrance. *What?* He could see the outline of a girl sitting in the chair. *Who was in the chair?!*

The sound of a soft, unexpected laugh gave him chills. Slade slowly turned, in search of the person laughing. Panic bubbled up inside him until he realized he was the freak who cackled hysterically. It took a minute to get himself under control, but when he did, he dropped that empty bottle. Surprisingly, it didn't shatter.

Slade marched across the room to the chair. There was rope on the floor next to it and a bit of blood smeared on the seat. *What the fuck?* Anika sat there and watched him fuck her friend. Did her period juices leak, making that mess? He turned around and sat on the chair, feeling his cock growing hard as he thought about her watching. That whole thing was NOT a hallucination. There was too much evidence.

That toothless whore was still downstairs, wasn't she? He could enjoy her while thinking about that look in Anika's eyes. Maybe he'd fuck the bitch's ass. He remembered tearing into it, and blood trickling down his cock and legs. His hand rubbed at the throbbing bulge in his pants.

Was the whore dead or not? It wouldn't be the first time he hallucinated a girl dying to find she wasn't dead. Or he could have kidnapped someone new again without remembering.

With a newfound excitement, he glanced at the clock before hurrying to the basement door. He had a little over an hour to kill. Hopefully, he'd be able to make it an enjoyable wait with the use of a doll.

Maybe later he should sit down and talk to Anika about the previous evening. She looked like she enjoyed it, and if that was the case, they could discuss changing the dynamics of their little family. He froze at the basement door, feeling sick. He should never expect something like that from Anika. That had to be his mind fucking with him.

What if he fucked his sister up and simply didn't remember it? She could have been crying earlier because she felt scared of him... too scared to tell him.

Slade pressed the buttons on the dial pad to unlock the door and entered the basement. He flicked on the light to find the room occupied. Thank goodness. He would need the stress relief.

It took a few moments to realize what he was staring at. With furrowed eyebrows, he took his time marching down the stairs as he processed the scene laid out before him.

"Nadine?" he whispered in horrified shock. "What happened to you?"

Through the massive ball gag in her mouth, she tried to scream in terror. Tears rolled from the corners of her eyes and down her temples. Her arms and legs were outstretched and trembling, cuffed to the restraints anchored to the concrete at the four corners of the mattress. He designed this set up for his little dolls, but he never intended to keep Anika's friend as one. She screamed, but the sound only came from her nose. Until she gagged on the ball and shuddered as she choked quietly. It took him a second to see beyond her nudity to notice one detail that even in his strangest hallucinated and mindless states, he wouldn't do. Possibly.

She had the handle of a toilet brush pushed up inside her. There was blood on the bed and the exposed bit of handle that protruded from her pussy. Those spiky spindles on the other end barely touched her thighs. After an entire night of struggling, those sharp nibs left scratches on her legs, some of which were bleeding.

He stared around the room cautiously as he approached the bed. Anika said the girl left, didn't she? Maybe he panicked, knowing she'd tell someone and trapped her down there. With nimble fingers, he undid the ball gag in her mouth.

Immediately, she began begging him to let her go, which was expected.

"Tell me what happened."

He reached down and carefully grabbed a hold of the toilet brush. He slid it partially out, though when she yelped in pain, he released it and looked up at her.

"Please, let me go. I won't tell anyone about anything. I promise."

He knew that was a lie. They all promised that same thing and meant it at the moment they uttered the oath, but it was all lies. He slid it a little further out, watching her squirm and whimper, still begging to be set free.

"How did you end up like this?"

"Anika!"

He froze, his eyes narrowing as he stared at the girl's big blue eyes. His hand clenched around the brush, nearly trembling.

"What did you just say?" Slade's voice was a dangerous hiss.

"Ow, it hurts. Slade, it hurts, stop!"

"I'll shove the other end of this up inside you if you don't explain yourself!"

Tears leaked from the corners of her eyes. The dumb doll probably just realized that he was far from some hero to rescue her or set her free.

"Because I laughed at her, after what you did. I said she deserved it for screwing with people..." He didn't understand what the fuck she was talking about. Her next words came out in a distraught wail. "She took my virginity with the toilet brush!"

Slade snorted, and the girl flinched, turning her face away from him as she quietly cried. He was sure he took her virginity in both holes. Bits and pieces of the previous night tried to rise in his mind, but he simply couldn't remember what happened. Slowly, his head cocked to the side and his fingers moved to touch her lips.

"Don't touch me! Pervert. You and your sister are nasty freaks!"

In a moment of rage, he pressed the ball gag against her mouth and had to use extreme force to get it in there. His anger built up like a white-hot fire.

Anika was NOT a freak. She was a good, sweet girl! He stood from the mattress and marched toward the exit, but that rage boiled over in a way he simply couldn't contend with. Slade turned around and ran back toward the little bitch.

The toes of his slipper covered foot hit the bristles of the toilet brush. He kicked it so hard, the entire length of the handle disappeared from sight. The girl didn't even scream. It was as if the pain went beyond measure and no sound could express it. Her eyes went wide. The girl seemed unable to find air. She lay there, finding it impossible to breathe.

"Just think, bitch. No one knows where you are. Cause you're a lying little cunt. Now, you're mine to torture and fuck. You better hope you die from internal bleeding today, because... I-Will-Make-You-Suffer."

He stormed up the stairs. He reached the top and dialed the code to exit. He marched out of the basement, slamming the massive door behind him, just as she caught her breath enough to wail in pain.

That fucking dumb whore! There was nothing wrong with his sister! She was perfect in every way!

Slade nearly made it to the front door when he paused, noticing the living room. *What the fuck?*

His house was practically destroyed. With grit teeth, his crimson eyes shifted to the clock. He had just enough time to put things to rights before he left to go meet Anika at the pool. He made his way across the room to where the couch stood on its end and sneered. The fucking TV got smashed!

Maybe he should check and see if his sister was already at the pool. Slade pulled out his phone and opened the app for his many cameras. The only camera he had at the pool was the one in the locker room pointed directly at Anika's locker. So, the chances of actually catching her there were rare.

After a few moments, he found the right footage, but saw the unexpected. She was already there at the school's pool, in the locker room and wearing her swimsuit. Her hair was wet, and water beaded on her skin. Anika lied down on a towel, perfectly framed by the viewfinder of his camera. She pulled her bottom lip into her mouth. Her fingers of one hand were rubbing her pussy while the other massaged her breast over that adorable pink swimsuit.

His cock was hard the instant he saw it. Maybe he could go downstairs and fuck that girl, anyway. It would make quite a mess, but he wasn't sure if he could resist his sister with how aroused that visual of her made him. No. He needed to be there. She'd go swimming without him and drown.

He barely made it to the front door when he pulled his phone out to watch Anika masturbate again. Nope. He wasn't going to make it. The thought of going to the pool and catching her in the act left a trace amount of hope swirling inside him. If he found her touching herself, he could use the footage to force her into a sexual relationship- NO! It was *ANIKA*!

Slade spun on his heels and bolted back into the basement. As he entered, he flicked on the light, probably blinding the little bitch who had been so savage about his sister.

"Guess what, whore? I have forty-five minutes to teach you how to be my doll."

She screamed out her nose, shaking her head quickly. Judging from the shrieks, she was attempting to make actual words to beg for her life. It wouldn't work. When his dolls pleaded, it simply disgusted him.

"You are actually the closest I've had to the real thing. Simply because you look and smell so much like her."

The girl fell silent. With wide eyes, she watched him descend at a lingering pace. His hand lightly trailed down the railing as he moved, emphasizing every second or third word by taking another step down.

"You will survive if you say, and do exactly as I tell you." He gave her the same speech he'd repeated multiple times. "Do you understand?"

The girl screamed, shaking her head. She trembled so hard that the metal chains attached to her leather cuffs rattled loudly. This girl had a fighting spirit. It would be fun to break her and remake her into a perfect little doll.

"Your new name is Anika."

Her eyes practically bulged out of her face. It was interesting to see the reaction of someone who knew him and his sister. Normally, his dolls had no reaction or connection to the name he gave them. This one knew the name had meaning.

He kneeled on the edge of the mattress and reached over with one hand, undoing the buckle that held it in place.

"What the fuck-" the girl started, but his hands wrapped around her throat and squeezed.

"The next thing you say will be your name." Her face turned purple, so he knew there wasn't much time before she lost consciousness. "You will have one chance."

His hands released their grip, which was immediately followed by her hacking and coughing. When the stupid girl caught her breath, she glared up at him with a quivering jaw.

"NAME!" he shrieked down at her, flecks of spit flinging at her face.

"Nay-deen."

"I was going to make love to you like you're Anika, but I guess I'll rape you like you're Nadine."

"Fuck you! You sick piece of-ugh humph!"

The rest of her insult became lost as he forced the gag back in.

"I don't need you to talk for this part."

Slade yanked out the toilet brush from her pussy, ignoring her agonized shrieks. He held it up and examined the blood coating the length of the handle.

"Look what you did to yourself." He brought the handle up for her to see, but when she turned her face away and closed her eyes, he dragged the bloody implement down the side of her face. "You'll see, blood makes a fantastic lube. You'll be glad for it when I take your ass's virginity after I fuck your pussy."

He pulled the front of his pants down to expose his cock, which was still limp. *What the fuck?!* He was always getting hard for absolutely no reason, and now he couldn't get it up.

What was wrong?! She wasn't Anika.

She refused to play his little game. Normally, he took his time to make them become his sister before fucking them. Maybe if he rubbed it against her, he would get in the mood a bit more and it would become hard. Or at least solid enough for penetration.

While climbing atop her, Slade buried his face into the girl's throat. He closed his eyes and rubbed himself against her. It was so slick that he had to look down. Blood covered his groin.

Nadine lay there, silently glaring at him with those judgmental eyes. Her jaw clenched tight around the gag as she fought the gasps of pain as he rubbed his limp dick against her damaged pussy.

Beep, Beep, Beep.

What the fuck? Slide shifted to his knees between her legs to pull his phone out of his pocket. The message on the phone tagging the alarm read. 'Swimming at Two.'

He had fifteen minutes, but still needed to remember there was travel time. He dropped the phone on the mattress next to Nadine and smirked at her.

"I have only a few minutes longer to torture you."

She closed her eyes tightly and turned her face away from him. A tear leaked from the corner of her eye, pooling in her long, blonde eyelashes. He focused on that tear and did his best to imagine it was Anika beneath him. Slade leaned down, bracing himself against her naked body. He licked her, tasting the salt of her pain.

It barely made him hard, but it was enough that he could force himself into her bloody pussy until he went limp again.

"Fuck this!" he snarled and wrapped his hand around his blood smeared cock.

His hand stuck to it from the blood, making him want to puke. He closed his eyes and massaged, rubbing the length of it, until he reached his climax. Slade quickly laid on top of the girl and pushed his slightly limp dick inside to fill her with his cum.

"You're gonna have my baby, whore. If you live that long." He whispered and received a wail of despair for his snide remark.

He crawled off the mattress, sneering down at his blood-soaked clothes. Slade stripped before chucking them in the garbage can in the corner. He went upstairs naked, leaving Nadine to weep in the basement. She was alone, helpless and soon she'd realize cooperation would ensure she would extend her lifespan.

Once upstairs, he paused, staring around his house. What the fuck happened here? Was he robbed? Slade didn't have anything really valuable, so he decided it would be best to get ready and deal with this when he got back.

It took him all of ten minutes to shower and find some clean clothes. Once ready, he grabbed his keys and hurried out the door. He left his house in that disastrous state to go be with his sister.

15

SIBLING LOVE
Anika Darling

With the time of her beloved brother's arrival coming close, she figured she'd set things up. Nearly every piece of her plan had fallen into place. Well, far from it, but she'd claim the events that weren't her doing as her own, anyway. After some time of swimming, the alarm she set on her phone dinged loudly to tell her time was nearly done. Slade was nothing if not punctual. It helped that the previous night she set an alarm on his phone.

She carefully climbed from the pool. Every form of exertion sent twinges of agony across her body. It was worth it. Anika didn't mind being in pain. In fact, a part of her enjoyed it. The searing across her body reminded her she was indeed alive. Sometimes she felt so numb that the only way to know that she wasn't dead was to cause pain. To herself or others.

Anika carefully made her way to the changing room, dragging her bag behind her. She pulled the towel out and set it on the bench. Near where Slade had his camera was a window, which had gray material over it so no one could see in, but it would allow the natural light through. She set up picture frames all along the ledge so that they were easy to notice. She used the school's darkroom and developed them herself. The images were all different sizes and encased in decorative frames. They were stills cut from Slade's own footage. Many of which had to be deleted for his own sanity, just in case he saw the videos.

Her full lips pulled into a tight smile as she repositioned the last photo. When viewed correctly, they would be like a dedicated timeline to his past, hopefully clearing things up for him. Limping to her bag, she took her time as she pulled out her swimsuit. If he came in and suspected that she'd already been in the pool, he'd flip instead of noticing any of her display.

The centerpiece of this masterful display was her own body. She spread her towel on the floor, knowing that if he looked through the camera, he would see only her in the position she placed herself. She folded her empty bookbag and set it up to act as a pillow.

She whimpered timidly when she crouched, attempting to put her swimsuit on. Bending over made her asshole pucker from the stress of the motion. It felt like a hot knife was being rammed inside her repeatedly with every motion. The agony was pure bliss. It was a tragic and wonderful reminder of the previous night's events.

With her specially selected outfit on, she carefully laid down on her towel, facing the hidden camera. Anika drew her bottom lip into her mouth and began rubbing herself, while allowing her eyes to sweep across the picture frames. Each time her gaze landed on the last image, she mentally flinched.

It took all her focus to keep from orgasming while she rubbed at her clit. The tight nylon of her swimsuit warmed at her touch and allowed a tickle of sensation through. Her other hand massaged her breasts, trying to pinch her hardened nipples, but her fingers would just slide across the skin tight material. Three times she came close to finishing and had to press her fingers hard to her clit and wait out the mounting orgasm. She stayed perfectly still as the tension radiating up from her pussy and across her stomach gradually declined. It allowed the throbbing pleasure to pass her by in a distant thrumming until she started the cycle again. He needed to hurry, or she'd cum without him.

"What the fuck?" she heard the most familiar voice echoing

into the large space from behind her. "Anika, stop touching yourself... What the hell?!"

At that point, stopping wasn't really an option. Her insides clenched just from hearing his voice. She let a moan escape her throat and closed her eyes, continuing her masturbation. Judging from the second, 'what the hell', he must have spotted the display she created across the window ledge.

She heard his sneakers squelching on the floor with each step he took. Slowly, he drew closer to the images, until he came into her sight line. Just looking at him made her pussy clench. The tension caused a shot of pain to radiate from her ass. His dark crimson eyes flashed from the photos to her face and back. They barely glanced down to where her hand continued to massage her clit through her swimsuit.

"What the fuck is this?"

"What do you think it is?"

"I didn't do this!" he picked up a framed image from the beginning of the timeline that clearly hosted him fucking her on his computer chair.

Over the past nine months, she'd been planning this moment. Every detail was perfect. All he needed to do was accept his fate. She'd do anything for him. She'd proven that repeatedly.

"No. *We* did." Her clarification was more for his sake than hers.

She watched as her dear, sweet, yet deranged brother processed the display before him. He must have recognized some of his victims who were also a feature. There were pictures of some of his most gruesome acts with them, like when he ripped out that last girl's teeth. Anika was right there. It was Anika that the doll had bitten, but by the next day, he didn't seem to remember and neither did the girl. Or Anika would have killed her sooner. She helped him kill almost every one of his dolls, but he had no recollection.

"I don't understand. I never touched you," he murmured as his fingers touched an image of them fucking on top of one of his victims while Anika strangled the life from the woman's body.

She moaned while slipping the straps from her shoulders and pulled it down, so the hem rested just above her nipple. Her entire body tingled in a rush that was impossibly overwhelming, though she stopped touching herself, because she didn't want to cum unless Slade was inside her.

He looked over his shoulder at her with furrowed eyebrows, as if he couldn't believe his own eyes. The poor fool was practically trembling, though she hoped it was from arousal and not self-loathing. He looked back at the pictures, and she wished the window would reflect his features. While he remained distracted, Anika removed her bathing suit. She winced in pain, but did her utmost to ignore it. Now was not the time for her to bitch out. All her hard work was coming to fruition.

"Last night?" a husky whimper echoed from him.

"It was wonderful," she assured him, not wanting him to freak out about causing her so much agony.

"Anika," he whispered, still not turning around to face her. "You do not know how bad I want you, but it's so wrong."

"I've already had you, again and again." Her lips pulled into a deviant smirk. "I want you to remember fucking me this time."

"You know about my memory problems?"

"I know everything, Slade." She already felt annoyed that he hadn't turned to face her. "I know more than you, and if you fuck me again, I'll tell you everything."

He whipped around to stare at her as she added, "You have all those burning questions, and I know how to soothe you."

His expression shifted when he found her completely naked with her legs spread wide; waiting for him. The surprise and desire on his features and the way his cheeks turned rosy were delicious. She saw his throat muscles flex as he swallowed. He wanted her, too. He just needed the right push... as usual.

"Doesn't it look yummy?" she whimpered, using two fingers to push the lips of her pussy apart, hoping to encourage him.

"I- it's wrong Anikaaaa."

He was losing his resolve. Just the way he whined her name told her as much. He knew her body, every curve, and each crevasse. The stupid man just needed to know it while he was in the right state of mind. He'd break eventually.

"Is it? I'm legal now. Have been for a month. Come now, sweet boy, you won't forget this time. I promise, I won't let you."

He took a step forward, but paused, making her wait. Damn it! She shifted her fingers so her middle one could massage in gentle circles around her clit, shifting it around. Maybe if she made it dance for him, he'd realize how hard with desire it had become. Anika moaned quietly, lifting her bottom from the towel. Her bottom clenched from the movement, forcing Anika to gasp in pain. Sweat trickled from her temple, but her skin and hair were still moist from swimming, so it wouldn't be that noticeable. With how torn up her asshole was, sex was going to hurt like a bitch, but she needed to hide that pain, or he'd never fuck her sober again.

"No more dolls, Slade."

Anika demanded, watching the guilty expression build up on his face. That might be the way to get him to cooperate.

"I'm right here. The one you've wanted all along. For all these months, you've played with those dolls. It's time for the real thing."

His jaw clenched. If she wasn't careful, he'd turn volatile. So, she moaned and began vigorously fingering herself while using her free hand to pinch and pull on her nipple hard enough to hurt before moving on to the other. The friction made them hard, and in her opinion, so much more desirable.

"Fuck me. I need you. You promised to take care of me, but you're not. I want you. I need you so bad!" Anika practically screamed, with tears leaking from the corners of her eyes, before she gave another throaty moan for emphasis.

Anika closed her eyes tightly and turned her face away, giving a quiet whimper. She nearly yelped as something landed atop her. Anika froze in her movements with her arm trapped. His weight atop her put pressure on her asshole, making that sensation of tearing flesh return. She had never felt a pain like being ass fucked with no preparation. It was impossibly painful.

"I love you, Anika." Slade growled, kissing up and down the side of her neck.

His icy touch sent chills across her flesh. Knowing that he was in his own mind and still touching her sent a wave of excitement across her body. More! MORE! Her hands searched his body for every curve with such enthusiasm, as if for the first time. She gasped out in surprise as his mouth opened wide. He bit her throat, almost hard enough to make her struggle to get away. Her hands balled into fists and pushed against his chest, but he didn't move. The man was like a feral animal when he snarled and grabbed her wrists, pinning them above her head. He pulled his face away to stare down at her with those dark crimson eyes, so full of fiery lust.

"Tell me the truth of it all." He purred down at her, rubbing his hard cock against her pussy. "Set my mind free."

"Fuck me." Anika could feel the heat of his cock through his jogging pants driving her crazy with a maddening desire for it to enter her body and pleasure them both.

She spread her legs wider to grant him easier access. All he needed to do was pull down the front of his pants and slide it into her. She dug her heels into the concrete and lifted her hips to push herself against him. His expression suddenly changed, making her nervous.

"Fuck." He growled and shifted his weight, but before he could pull away, she locked her ankles behind him.

He would not be running away!

"Promise." He barely murmured before his lips pressed to hers.

She felt him adjust, and then she felt the pressure of his bare cock touching her hole. It seemed as if he was struggling with himself once more. She wiggled her hips in desperate impatience.

"Do it."

"Condom."

His hips tried to pull away, but she had him trapped. Anika didn't care about protection. He was hers forever, so it wouldn't mean a thing.

"It won't matter."

"It does."

"Stupid. We've been having unprotected sex for months." His eyes narrowed, and she spoke, then tensed her legs to pull him against her. "Just fuck me."

She could feel his entire body trembling. His ability to resist would soon dissolve and he would fuck the hell out of her like the beast he was. His cock touched her entrance and her mouth watered almost as much as her pussy.

The damn coward had other plans. "Can we do this at home?"

She grit her teeth in annoyance before hissing, "No."

Anika wiggled her hips to encourage him to enter her. The movement was a regrettable decision because her asshole puckered tightly, causing a shot of pain to ripple across her body.

"Why not?" His features darkened, making her feel that ever familiar anxiety creep up inside her.

"Because we've never done it here." She pouted, forcing tears to well in her eyes, knowing how it drove him crazy. "Please. I need you inside me. Don't you love me?"

He sighed, pressing his cock a little harder against her tense entrance. The pain and pleasure as his dick stretched her around its girth was immeasurable. The moment his head entered, he went balls deep in one smooth motion that left her gasping for air. Slade's hot breath caressed her cheek as he panted lightly. She opened her eyes to see his eyebrows had drawn down over his closed eyes. He looked so beautiful. Her fingers slipped up his back, under his shirt, desperate to feel more of him. Suddenly, his eyes opened and narrowed as he stared down at her in confusion.

"I don't remember doing it anywhere." His voice was flat and emotionless, as if something had snapped inside him.

This was not what she imagined it being like the first time they did it when he would actually be of sound mind. He was suddenly distant and calculating. The change in him made him completely different from the warm and sweet brother she'd always admired.

"You will this time," she promised, giving him an encouraging smile before lifting her head from the ground to kiss him.

He pulled his face away, which only applied more pressure to his cock, buried deep inside her. "How can you be so sure?"

"Cause I know everything. Now fuck me."

Slade sneered and pulled his cock out. She clenched her legs, but he was stronger than he looked. His hand pushed on her lower stomach as he forced his way out of her.

"Enough Anika!" he snapped, and she finally unlocked her legs from behind him.

He climbed off of her and stood up. Slade quickly yanked his sweatpants up over his dick and raised an eyebrow at her before crossing his arms. She grit her teeth in rage and frustration before watching him march toward the door. His voice rang out from in the large open changing space.

"Clean up your shit and meet me in the car."

That fucking bastard!

16

TRUTH BRINGS PEACE
Slade Darling

After the fluorescence in the school's pool building had tamed his vision, the midday sun burned his eyes. The large red door sprang shut behind him on its own, though he barely noticed as he made his way across the parking lot. His cock angrily bobbed around inside his sweatpants, as if desperate to taste Anika's hot pussy one more time.

He clicked the button on his keys, which unlocked the doors. Sundays were always dead quiet, as if no one wanted to be out and about. Was it even Sunday?

His heart still thundered in his chest along with an agonizing pain which only worsened when thoughts of his sister floated up. He needed to face the fact that she wasn't this sweet and innocent creature he thought she was.

The door to the building flung open violently. It rammed into the wall behind it, loud enough the bang echoed across the secluded parking lot. While Anika stomped her way toward the car, the red door slammed shut behind, making her flinch and turn back.

She wore her school uniform. The short skirt flickered around her thighs as the wind picked up the pace. He licked his lips, wanting that material to move upward a little more than the breeze allowed. She saw him watching and gave a warm smile, though the way she walked didn't alter with the apparent change in mood. The girl was practically stomping as she made her way to the car.

Maybe she was a lot more like him than he ever thought. His hands trembled, so he stuffed them into his pockets. The boner between his thighs was massive and very noticeable as it bobbed around with every movement.

Anika opened the car door to the back seat and shoved her bag. Its contents clattered loudly as it landed on the floor back there. She closed the door and turned toward him, crossing her arms beneath her small breasts. Her eyes trailed down his body, taking a moment to examine his groin. She licked her lips, as if appreciating the erection, before smirking at him.

"We *are* going to fuck again."

"Why?"

She shook her head slowly with that damn smirk growing before turning on her heels to stroll away. He watched her closely while she made a wide circle around the back of her vehicle, keeping their gazes locked. She grinned playfully before climbing into the passenger seat of the car. Now that he knew they had fucked several times, and his sister seemed screwed up to begin with, he kept letting the idea of 'what if' pop into his head. The massive hard-on, demanding attention didn't help him combat the intrusive thought in the slightest.

After several breaths to calm himself, he realized that with the angle he stood at and the height of the car, if she looked out the driver's side window, all she would see was that massive boner. There was no removing temptation for him, because he'd have to climb into the car with her, then go home with her. At least, if he could resist until he got home, he could fuck that doll in the basement. Maybe they could return to the way things were before.

Slade climbed into the driver's seat and threw his gear into reverse to pull out of the parking spot. He wasn't even outside of the parking lot, and Anika had her hand touching him. Just her cool touch radiating through his pants, where her hand innocently resting on his leg was enough to make his cock bounce and throb painfully. No. She wasn't innocent anymore. He needed to remember that.

"How long?" he croaked out, though his voice didn't really want to work.

"What?" Her hand slid dangerously close to his groin.

"You know what."

"I told you, I'd give you answers if you willingly fuck me."

The way she phrased that made the entire thing seem suspicious. Willingly? Was he unwilling? Apparently, they'd done it several times in the past. Was he unwilling before?

"Then answer my questions."

"Okay." Her hand moved to his dick as she gave her single word response.

His hands clenched on the steering wheel as he struggled to keep his focus and the vehicle on the road. The moment her hand touched his shaft through his pants, he spluttered pre-cum, dampening the gray material around the tip of his dick. Her fingers slid up and down the length, comfortable enough with touching him it seemed she'd done it a thousand times before.

"Why the fuck won't it go away?" He growled, frustrated at how his body betrayed him.

"Because you want me, and your dick is making that clear."

Her tone was playful and bordered on musical, but he could almost taste the lie in her words. She slid her hand up and down the length, and a tiny part of him wished his pants were nonexistent. He was so distracted by her movements that he took a wrong turn. And then another. Maybe he was subconsciously trying to prolong the car ride.

"Planning on a pleasant country drive?"

"Sure."

He let himself drive straight out of town. Anika flipped up the divider between the two front seats to make it a single long bench seat.

Click.

"Anika, seatbelt."

He heard it retract into its compartment. She was being so disobedient! This behavior was completely unlike her. At any rate, how could he say anything about who she was?

She snorted loudly and leaned forward across the bench. Thank goodness he has such ridiculously long legs. In order for him to drive, he had the bench seat moved far enough back to give his legs room. That ensured there was lots of room for her body to move around easily.

She pressed her mouth to the wet spot on his pants. It felt as if her lips were kissing the head of his dick until she breathed out. Humid breath tickled his dick through his pants, making him gasp loudly. He hadn't noticed how much faster he drove with every second of her taunting. His foot tapped the brake, trying to slow down.

"Don't slow down." She looked up at him through her long, blonde eyelashes. "I like the rush."

Bossy little brat. That was his fault. He raised her to know he would do his best to ensure she had everything she wanted. He turned her into this person, and he never even noticed until it was too late.

Her fingers curled over the waistband of his pants, making his stomach tense. Those cool fingers tickled his skin just under the waistband for a moment, as if she was waiting for permission.

He didn't deny her access, but didn't grant it either. In fact, he bit his bottom lip, waiting in desperate anticipation for whatever Anika did next. She pulled the material down so his dick could finally be free of its confines. Her fingers lifted it from its resting place against his thigh so it could stand fully erect in all its towering glory.

"I love your dick so much." Her purring words came an instant before her mouth engulfed his entire cock, right down to the base.

He moaned softly, moving a hand from the wheel to the back of her neck. It felt so good that he wanted to close his eyes and bask in that glorious heat engulfing him whole. She moaned, sending a vibration down the entire shaft. The hand holding his pants open rotated so she could massage his balls. The back of her hand kept the waistband of his pants from slapping her in the face as she worked.

Her head bobbed wildly, while she used her tongue, lips and throat to pleasure him. Refraining from cumming was impossible with the insane waves of pleasure that washed over him. A part of Slade hoped that if he came, his cock would lose its vigor and this entire thing would pause for a bit to give him time to process the situation.

The only reason he put off finishing was because an entirely different part of him wanted to prolong the moment. He had spent so long dreaming and fantasizing about his moment. It had been nearly a year since the first time he had an inkling of desire for the girl who clearly felt the same.

Too bad he had no proper control over his body. Cum exploded out of his dick, making her gag loudly. She choked, retching, before pulling away to stare down gleefully. She wiped her mouth with her forearm before returning it to the tip. The sucking sensation resumed as she drank every ounce of cum his dick could provide for her.

"Now you need to tell me the entire story. Everything you know. Tell me what happened."

"I said fuck me."

He was still hard. His eyes flashed down to his cock. He hadn't meant it as an invitation, but that was how she took it. Anika crawled over to him and slipped her leg across his lap, wedging it between the edge of his seat and the door. Lucky for her, there was quite the gap there in the old car.

He was quite tall, so seeing over her head was easy, especially because of how short she was. The gasp that escaped his lips wasn't on purpose. It tumbled from his lips along with a timid moan as she gently rocked herself against him. He always imagined that if she gave her virginity to him, it would be tender and slow, very much like this. But to his dismay, she was far from a virgin.

"Fuck," he growled, feeling himself about to cum again. "Why?! How am I so fucking hard?"

"I gave you something for it."

She laughed as if it was some sort of grand joke. It was almost like his cock just couldn't get enough.

"Gave me something? How, when?"

"All the time." She gently bit his nipple through his shirt, making him wince.

"Why?"

"To make you compliant, silly." His jaw clenched, hearing her answer so nonchalantly. "Think about it. We would not be fucking right now if I hadn't. You'd still be whining about wanting me while doing nothing about it." He suddenly lost his appetite for conversation. How long had she been giving him stuff to make him *compliant*? What did she give him? His throbbing boner spoke volumes.

"When did this start?" His throat was so dry his voice came out husky.

17

Anika's Darling
Anika Darling

This was what she was building toward. All this time, ever since he fucked her friend instead of her. Torren got to experience what she had been desperate to have. After that, she started drugging him with her antipsychotics to see what it would do. When there were minor changes, Anika did a lot of serious research into over-the-counter meds and what combining certain medications would do to him. Then the experiments really took off.

After several months, she found the perfect cocktail that would fuck him right out of his tree. It made him pliable and easier to manipulate. It wasn't enough, but it was a good start.

She would leave things with her scent in places he could find them and made carefully planned, innocent-appearing advances to make him see her sexually. Slade was so hyper focused on protecting her, it made it impossible for him to see that she was not a totem of purity and innocence for him to prize.

Her father had psychotic tendencies and forced Slade to help him torture several victims. It messed with the boy's head and during a family vacation, he nearly drowned her for fun. When she didn't react, he spared her when they were children. His mentality toward her changed, and she became the one untouchable creature who no one could touch. That desperate desire of his to protect her was destroying any chance she had of having him on an intimate level and something needed to be done about it or she'd go insane.

Simply drugging him, giving him cocktails of medication in his food, and drink wasn't always going to be enough. She needed to make him think he was more insane than he was, so he'd have a scapegoat for horrible behavior. Eventually, he abducted his first victim, falling into the pattern her father led him down as a child. She saw a change in him, which she wasn't expecting.

The mindless idiot coped by wiping out entire chunks of memory. So she did the same by erasing his paranoid camera footage. There were times he was so out of his mind she could help torture and torment the dolls, but he'd forget. In order to ensure his mental stability after his derailment, she murdered several of his whore dolls and left him thinking he did it. The last one was an accident.

When Anika went downstairs, suspecting that the doll was already dead, she found the woman untied and heavily hallucinating. The girl was likely sharing Slade's food and that night she had put certain mushrooms in the sauce. They got into a scuffle at the top of the stairs and if it weren't for Anika's strength from swim training, the dumb bitch would have escaped.

The memory of killing his doll resurfaced in her mind, making her wetter than she already was. His glorious cock filled her. And this time, he wasn't high or drugged with anything aside from some little blue pills she stole from Torren's dad.

The pressure and pain from her ass were excruciating, which was why she moved so slowly. If she didn't fuck him now while his resolve wavered, she'd lose her chance. Every piece had fallen into place. After all the work she did to get to this moment, she wasn't going to let it slip by.

Grinding her hips against him, she basked in the moment's ambiance. Everything seemed to be on a time lapse with every second passing by in slow motion. Her small gasps in pain and pleasure made his cock throb and pulse inside her. She could feel his pre-cum warming her insides.

She realized when her eyes flashed out to the surrounding forest she did not know where they were. Maybe it was for the best. He probably didn't either, because of how distracting the pleasure of her pussy was for him. She continued to roll her hips while resting her head on his chest, simply to enjoy the feeling of him inside her.

18

Repetition and Redemption
Slade Darling

Anika leaned back slightly, trying to reach a hand down to rub her clit. He made an annoyed sound and used his forearm to press her body against his. From the corner of his eye, he saw her features light up, so he coldly hissed.

"Don't touch the wheel. You'll make us crash."

"You're not really fucking me if I'm doing all the work."

"Shut up and move your ass, or I'll fuck that instead."

Her face turned pale, and he suddenly had flashbacks to the night before. The last picture on the windowsill in the change room was him fucking her over the back of the couch. It was his sister's ass he fucked with such brutal intensions. His anger turned inward and became directed at himself. She'd been drugging him! Was it causing all these mental issues he'd had lately? If he asked, would she admit it?

"How long?" His voice sounded throaty, as if his entire skeleton clutched tightly around his insides.

"Hmmm. After you fucked Torren."

She started drugging him after he fucked her friend. That was around the time he started having mood swings and would pass out from exhaustion at random times. Shortly after that, he started lusting after his precious little sister. The moment he realized he wanted her, he had to find an outlet, so he took after her father and the lessons the old man taught him. He started abducting and hurting women.

Before he even realized it was happening, tears leaked from the corners of his eyes. He wasn't sad or anything, they just came out on their own. He had so much pent-up fear, pain and self-loathing that it seemed to trickle out from his eyes.

She frowned, tilting her head to the side while watching him closely. He swallowed reflexively and cocked an eyebrow, glancing down at her briefly from the corner of his eye. She looked so beautiful with her eyebrows pulled down over those dark blue eyes. Could she actually feel confused about his reaction?

"Anika." His voice cracked loudly as he tried to whisper. "Why didn't you just talk to me?"

She lifted herself until his cock had almost slipped from her tight little pussy. The chilly wind in the vehicle cooled the moistened flesh that was freshly exposed to it. Her warm lips touched his cheek in an affectionate kiss, followed by a second and third. Her lips destroyed the trail of tears. Her cool fingers tangled in his hair at the nape of his neck.

She whispered to him, with her lips touching his earlobe. "Would you have fucked me?"

Before he could answer, she slid herself back down. The fire of her insides suddenly wrapped around him. The feeling of her engulfing his cock made him gasp once again, basking in the glory of his dearest little sister. Anika's small swimmer's body pressed against him, making him wish they were both naked.

"I would have gotten you help," he barely mumbled in a hushed whimper.

His hands clenched on the steering wheel so hard his knuckles whitened. Would he have gotten her help? Or would he have given into temptation and fucked her as he was currently doing?

"You already have me on anti-psychotics... Well, you think you do. I've never actually taken any of them."

His brows furrowed as he thought back to all the times that he gave her the medication. He even placed it on her tongue. Did she never actually swallow a single one? His teeth clenched. He'd been giving her these pills for years, since she was at least thirteen, and she'd even requested increases in her dosages several times. She had a hoard of pills hidden somewhere. No. no, she probably didn't. Not any more... because she'd been feeding them to him and using his new instability to manipulate and torture him.

It was possible that they were just like their parents. The thought made him feel sick. He always felt that the only reason his narcissistic mother wanted to kill the children along with herself and her husband was because she couldn't stand the thought of the pair outliving her.

"Slade. Please don't be cross," she whimpered, pulling her head away from his chest, so he could see the tears welling in her eyes.

Fuck. Her tears always enraged him for two polar opposite reasons. First, she never cried as a child, even when he drowned her when she was 6. She didn't even whimper. And second, watching someone else's pain turned him on. He was so focused on protecting her that when she cried, he'd become aroused, which was immediately followed by rage and self-loathing.

"Anika." He watched her lick her lips and smile deliciously at him. "Kiss me."

"You won't be able to see the road."

"I'll risk it." A numbness spread across his body.

The desperate girl didn't need to be told again. She firmly planted her lips on his. Her slender arms circled the back of his neck, deepening the furtive kiss. He did not wait for her lips to part before he pushed his tongue into her mouth. When her tongue met his, he retreated to suckle on hers. He watched her eyes close tightly as she basked in their embrace and combined flavors.

Slade released the wheel with one hand and used it to wrap tightly around her, pulling her hard down atop him and plowing his cock the deepest inside her it could go. She practically yelled into his mouth from the pain as he stretched her to fit him.

Bracing her tiny body against his, Slade used his free hand to spin the wheel and force the car off the road. Anika screamed, breaking off the kiss to turn to see where they were going.

The last time they soared off the side of this bridge, he was unconscious, so he didn't remember that flying sensation. Anika had been awake when their parents drove off this same bridge to kill the family.

There was a moment where he had a feeling of weightlessness before the vehicle plummeted to the water's surface. His cock hardened with the exhilaration of a rapid descent at the same time her pussy squeezed him to the brink of agony. In the mere seconds of flight, he wrapped his free arm around Anika, holding her tightly to him. Her screaming reverberated through him to the core, making his cock practically thunder with blood flow while his cum filled her.

Slamming into the water flung them around, but thankfully, his grip on Anika kept her from getting too hurt. The car sank rapidly, far faster than he remembered his parent's car sinking. Possibly because he had the windows open, and they didn't. Or maybe it was because he was a child and the trauma made it feel like everything was slower.

"Fuck! Shit, Slade! We gotta get out of here." Her tiny body struggled, grabbing at his door handle, but he had the door locked.

The water was already reaching his knees. The more she wiggled around, the tighter she became. He moaned quietly, cumming again. The last thing he did in this life was cum in his baby sister's tight little pussy. Their death was going far better than he could have imagined.

His heart thundered in his ears as the water rose above his hips. There was a glimmer of thought where he was glad to keep his cock rammed inside the tight warmth of Anika's hot pussy. She kept it safe for him.

"Fuck!!!" Anika shrieked, but when Slade chuckled, she froze and glared at him. Her voice was a hissing whisper. "Let me go."

He smiled.

The blood drained from her face before her hands moved to his chest so her nails could gouge at his skin through his shirt. Her insides squeezed him so hard that he moaned, pulling his bottom lip into his mouth. She clenched around him tight enough; he was sure her body was on the verge of an orgasm.

"I love you, Anika." He whispered softly, leaning forward to kiss her.

When his lips brushed hers, he felt her insides pulsate around him as her arousal increased. He pulled his lips away, but instead of staring at her, he moved his face forward to her ear. He licked up the side of her neck before sucking on her earlobe. He was sure his breaths would sound so loud as he panted from the adrenaline rush. His heart pounding was the loudest noise and a stark contrast to the eerie silence of the car filling with water.

"I'd love to fuck you in the water... fuck you for the rest of my life."

"You're insane." Her voice trembled beautifully.

"Admiring your accomplishment?" He licked up the curve around the side of her ear and when she didn't respond, he added, "I won't let you go. Ever. So, you may as well take what you wanted so badly, and fuck the life out of me."

Her insides tightened around him as if gradually coming to accept this turn of events. With every word he said, the car inched downward in the water. She ground her hips and his hands moved to her ass cheeks, prying them apart as he squeezed and pulled her hard against him. He knew very well how painfully torn her asshole was, and that movement was probably absolute hell for her. *Good.*

Feel everything Anika! everything you wanted! You are getting your prize.

He would be only hers for all eternity, and she would return the favor. They'd enter the gates of the afterlife swaddled in each other's arms. This was his last loving gesture to his beautiful little sister. Romance wasn't dead. It was dying with them in that car ride to the abyss.

The water had increased enough he had to lift his bottom from the seat to keep her head above the surface. This was the last few seconds they had with oxygen. He needed to say something worth remembering.

"Out of all the times I killed you, this is my favorite."

He took a deep breath of air a moment before the water pushed out the last of the oxygen in bubbles to the surface. The car torpedoed downward. He pulled her tight against him, holding on as they sank to the bottom. His ears popped painfully, making him close his eyes, until they jarringly hit the bottom.

The first thing he saw was his sister's pale, pretty face. Her hair flowed around behind her like a mythological mermaid. She was such a creature of unfathomable beauty.

A few small bubbles leaked from Anika's nose, drawing Slade's attention to the smile on her lips. Maybe she accepted this plan of his. He pressed his mouth to hers, basking in the feel of her. She returned his kiss, but as she pulled away, she smiled again before rolling her hips, making his cock rub deep inside her.

He moaned and lost a few bubbles of air. Oops. He didn't want to lose consciousness before Anika, but his head was already pounding. That smile she had on her face made him feel sick with worry. He let go of her ass and slid her hands up her back to hold her in a tight hug. This was it. The last few moments of their lives. They should have died ten years before, with their twisted parents, but he was making up for his mistake of rescuing them.

Unsure of how much longer he'd make it. He closed his eyes and let his body convulse hard while pushing a few air bubbles out of his nose. Once he laid still, releasing his grip on her, Anika pulled away. He heard a soft thump as her hands grabbed the edges of his window.

Exactly as he suspected. Anika, the swim team champion, was waiting for him to die so she could simply swim out of the wreck and make her way to the surface.

She was about to pull herself out and escape dying with him! He wrapped his arms so tight around her it was as if he was trying to squeeze the life from her. Slade slammed her back down against his massively hard cock. Clearly, it remained erect, resulting from the drugs she'd given him. His dick missed her pussy, and unfortunately for Anika, it slammed into her asshole.

The mischievous little bitch screamed in pure agony for a moment before clapping her hands to her mouth. She'd regret that loss of oxygen. Her face was incredibly red, though it turned purple around her mouth and nose. Slade was sure that he looked very much the same. Her hands came up as if launching forward to scratch his face. He released her body to catch her hands and pin them to the roof of the car as he rammed his hips forward once more, making sure he didn't slip out more than a few inches while they struggled.

There was no saying how much longer he could hold on. He put both her hands into one of his and moved his newly freed fingers down along her body. She twitched away from him, and he realized something. Apparently, she realized it as well. Her head shook with pleading eyes.

Slade moved his fingers to her ribs and gently dug them in and wiggled them. The last of Anika's air bubbled out and a moment of despair flashed across her ethereal features. Her change of expression was short-lived, because pain and panic flooded her face as she twitched and writhed while she drowned. A muffled garble of sound came from her body as she violently convulsed.

He had strangled a few of his dolls while fucking them. He enjoyed feeling their insides tense around his cock, but nothing compared to the sensations he received from her asshole as she fought for her life and failed. Once her death rattle was over, Slade kissed her temple and pulled her tightly against him. His hand moved to her neck, looking for a pulse, to be sure.

Nothing.

He undid his seatbelt, pulled her against him and carefully pushed his cock inside her pussy before buckling it back up so it would hold them together for all eternity. He pressed his mouth against her icy lips while forcing the last of the air from his lungs out of his nose.

Even during his death rattle, he barely moved, desperate to ensure they could remain locked together for all eternity.

www.ingramcontent.com/pod-product-compliance
Lightning Source LLC
LaVergne TN
LVHW010108170826
845678LV00012B/2296

* 9 7 8 1 7 3 8 8 4 6 9 0 0 *